Aiden knew their time had run out. So did Mack.

Aiden downshifted the gear two clicks while Mack threw open the door as wide as it would go. The second the truck went into Neutral, it started to roll. Just as Mack's hand wrapped around his arm.

The force was startling, but Mack pulled him out in one fluid move.

Aiden went to the edge of the road, fully ready to go into the trees, but he stopped short.

The trees were there, but so was a drop. The slope was significant enough that Aiden forgot Mack's instruction completely.

There was no way he could run down it. Even if he could have seen where the slope led, the journey to get there wouldn't be a fun ride.

There had to be another way.

There had to be another path.

There—

A hand, warm and strong, wrapped around Aiden's.

Then Mack was off the edge of the road in a flash.

Hand in hand, they ran as fast as they could and made their escape.

Dear Reader,

I'm so excited to be able to share Mack and Aiden with the world! I've always wanted to showcase a pure, fun love between two male characters and am beyond honored that Harlequin gave me the opportunity. Mack and Aiden have been living in my heart for years as the quiet bodyguard of mystery and the stylish hacker who is loudly himself. My favorite part about them, though, is how I pictured them before I ever had a plot. Mack always had his arms crossed over his chest, frowning and very much looking like he didn't want to be wherever he was, while Aiden was excitedly talking about something or other. Yet Mack never complained. In fact, good luck to anyone who tried to make him leave Aiden's side.

And, honestly, it was that simple, content feeling when I thought of them that made me want to see this dynamic couple use their differences as strengths while solving a dangerous mystery...and while falling in love.

I'm so grateful I can share them, and their story, with y'all. I hope you enjoy *Dangerous Recall*!

Happy reading!

Tyler Anne Snell

DANGEROUS RECALL

TYLER ANNE SNELL

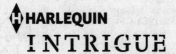

This book is for everyone who loves love. I hope you enjoy
Mack and Aiden as much as I did.

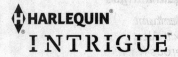

HARLEQUIN®

INTRIGUE™

Recycling programs
for this product may
not exist in your area.

ISBN-13: 978-1-335-59164-7

Dangerous Recall

Copyright © 2024 by Tyler Anne Snell

Harlequin Enterprises ULC
22 Adelaide St. West, 41st Floor
Toronto, Ontario M5H 4E3, Canada
www.Harlequin.com

Printed in Lithuania

MIX
Paper | Supporting
responsible forestry
FSC® C021394

Tyler Anne Snell lives in South Alabama with her same-named husband, their artist kiddo, four mini "lions" and a burning desire to meet Kurt Russell. Her superpowers include binge-watching TV and herding cats. When she isn't writing thrilling mysteries and romance, she's reading everything she can get her hands on. How she gets through each day starts and ends with a big cup of coffee. Visit her at www.tylerannesnell.com.

Books by Tyler Anne Snell

Harlequin Intrigue

Manhunt
Toxin Alert
Dangerous Recall

The Saving Kelby Creek Series

Uncovering Small Town Secrets
Searching for Evidence
Surviving the Truth
Accidental Amnesia
Cold Case Captive
Retracing the Investigation

Winding Road Redemption

Reining in Trouble
Credible Alibi
Identical Threat
Last Stand Sheriff

Visit the Author Profile page at Harlequin.com.

CAST OF CHARACTERS

Mack Atwood—Still angry at a tragedy from his past, this quiet bodyguard returns home to rest between work contracts with every intention of leaving again. It isn't until he unexpectedly meets a charming newcomer in danger that he decides that staying to protect him is his only option.

Aiden Riggs—Starting over again isn't hard for this former computer hacker. That is, until his past brings danger—and a dead body—right to his doorstep. With the help of the attractive yet cold bodyguard at his side, he must figure out a dangerous secret before it's too late.

Leighton Hughes—Aiden's ex-boyfriend and former colleague. His cryptic phone call sets all of the danger Aiden and Mack face into motion.

Goldie and Finn Atwood—The Atwood twins are quick to help Mack and Aiden whenever the need arises.

Ray Dearborn—Mack's childhood best friend, this medical examiner is eager to solve the recent murder in town.

Detective Winters—Deeply disliked by the Atwood family, this ace detective is more of a problem than help.

Chapter One

The nameless park a mile past the town crossroad was hands down the quiet pride and joy of the town of Willow Creek.

It wasn't much—there was no playground equipment, no intricate flower beds, no fountain or centerpiece that sparkled or stood out—but the greenery surrounding the half-acre plot of land more than earned the love of the town. It was called magic by most, a godsend by a few, because no matter what was happening in a person's life, the park always seemed to spare a moment of peace to those who visited. There was no rhyme or reason to it. No town lore or rumor that made it so. Yet, there wasn't a local who hadn't gone there at one time or another looking for some slice of soothing.

Which made the body found buried next to the big, knotted and knobby oak tree near the end of the simple walking path a shocking discovery. And, honestly, a shame to boot.

The park's peace had been invaded.

That was to speak nothing of the man murdered and hidden there.

Malcolm Atwood squatted down to get a better view of the makeshift grave. He was wearing the clothes he'd come from the airport in and was regretting not changing into something more comfortable before his way-too-early morning flight. He'd been in town less than a half hour and now he was staring at a dead man while wearing slacks and shining shoes.

It made an already not-right situation feel even more so.

Mack sighed out long and drew the attention of the young deputy standing a few feet from them. He'd already caught her flinch at the blood-soaked earth. It was her first homicide, he'd guessed. It was not Ray Dearborn's first. Medical examiner by day, childhood friend of Mack's since first grade, Ray had been at the feet of a dead body before. However, what was a first was calling Mack in to see it, too.

"Usually when I come back into town you're offering me a drink, not the dead," he said, crouching to get a better look at the partially uncovered man between them. Mack guessed he might not have been found so soon had it not stormed the night before. The ground around them had been washed out by the rain. "I also think you've forgotten that my job revolves around protecting the living. This is a little out of my bounds."

Ray stopped whatever notes he'd been taking on his clipboard and tried to be cheeky.

"Maybe this is my way of forcing you to be social," he said.

Mack snorted, because it wasn't exactly outside the scope of what Ray might do. The saying that introverts don't make friends, they only get adopted by extroverts was an accurate way to describe how their relationship started. Now in their early thirties, that dynamic hadn't changed.

"Considering you know where I live and what time I was coming in today, I'm guessing this isn't a social call." Mack met his friend's eye. "Tell me."

Ray let out a sigh that rivaled Mack's. He at least managed to look apologetic before he spoke again.

"The almighty Sheriff Boyd told me to reach out," he admitted. "He was with me when I first got on scene and kind of got squirmy when I said I didn't recognize this victim. This is the first murder in Willow Creek since he took over. I think he wants us to wrap this up before anyone else gets word of it."

"And why did he want *me* here?"

Mack still wasn't getting how the dead one and his one made two.

Ray put up his gloved hands in defense. He'd never been a man to be sheepish, but he looked close to it.

"He knows about your face thing," he answered. "And before you go throwing rocks, it wasn't me who spilled the beans. I mean, seriously, how many times have I heard you complain to me that you're not some kind of computer or personal database? Why would I purposefully incur that kind of wrath again by blabbing to the sheriff about it?"

An old feeling of anger started to kick around. Mack wasn't unused to it. He'd been living alongside that feeling since the day the warehouse burned down. The day that his knack for remembering faces put him in his own personal hell. The anger that was always there but kept in check by the unending patience he'd inherited from his father.

Ray, whose father was often found singing karaoke at the local bar despite it not having a karaoke machine, swore before he made his guess.

"I'd say Deputy McCoy spilled the beans," he added. "He's really been sticking with the sheriff lately. Anything he can do to prove he's useful, I'm sure he'd jump at it. He was on shift this morning, so I'm sure if the sheriff men-tioned needing to identify a John Doe quick, he threw out your name. Though, let's be honest, almost everyone in town knows about your brainpower thing. He could have already found out."

Mack sucked on his teeth. He looked down at John Doe again.

"I wish you'd stop calling it a power," he told his friend. "Some people are just good at remembering things. I just happen to be good at remembering faces."

It was true—Mack had a thing about people, specifically remembering their faces. After seeing someone, his mind seemed to save them forever. He saw a face and it stuck in place.

It was one reason he was good at his current job.

Being able to do threat analysis for a client was a lot easier when you could bookmark all the people around them.

John Doe's face, however, wasn't familiar. It was an odd feeling for Mack, being in Willow Creek and seeing someone he didn't recognize. He had been born in town, lived in it with zeal until college and then, with a lot less enthusiasm, had come back to use his family's home as a base of operations. A place he came to when he needed a place to go, as his sister had disapprovingly said many times before.

If John Doe was a local, he'd managed to stay beneath the Mack Atwood radar all this time. An impressive but not impossible thing to accomplish.

Mack thought out loud now.

"Blond hair, dark from the dirt, nose with a crook in it from probably being broken once or twice, some stubble on his face, some freckles, too, and the upper body build of someone who took relative care of themselves by exercising and or a good diet…" Mack shook his head. "I've never seen him before. In person, print or online. I don't know who he is."

It wasn't the news Ray wanted to hear. It wasn't like Mack enjoyed giving it. For Ray to call him to a crime scene had taken a lot for the man, but the new sheriff was known for his brashness and his charm and had no doubt used both to get the medical examiner to call in a civilian. It was probably called a favor, too. Sheriff Boyd seemed to like asking for those.

Being the favor himself, Mack had mixed feelings about not being able to come through.

"Sorry," he added, standing tall and wiping the dirt from the knees of his slacks. "Reelection optics for the sheriff aside, I know you're not a fan of homicide investigations. It would have been nice to make this part easier for you at least."

Ray waved him off.

"Don't apologize for something most people wouldn't even try. My phone is filled with contacts, and I don't think any of them would have beelined it to a crime scene after an early morning of flying. The detectives can deal with this. Me, too. I am a big boy, after all. You've seen my house, right? It's as intelligent and suave as me."

Mack snorted.

"Last I checked, your bedroom has a section of it dedicated to comic books. Comic books you've never opened."

Ray rolled his eyes.

"Hey, considering I deal with dead people all day, why don't you cut a man slack for having a hobby that brings him some joy? Plus, collecting is the new it thing. Everyone has something they want to preserve, but also, show off. I'm human like that, Mr. Brainpower."

Mack couldn't help but chuckle at that.

"I'll take your word for it, Dr. Dearborn."

A moment of silence bloomed between them as both took another regretful look at John Doe. The sound of car doors closing in the distance brought Ray back first. He nodded over his shoulder.

"That would be either our shining Detective Winters or the CSI crew," he said. "If you want to avoid them, I'd get going now."

Mack didn't need to be told twice.

"Good luck with this. Call me later."

Ray said he would, and Mack left the simple path and instead made a circle around to the parking lot with haste. Sure enough, a new cruiser was in the small lot. Detective Winters was nowhere to be seen.

It was a stroke of good luck that Mack wanted to capitalize on. He was in his truck and on the road within the minute. There he had been trying to avoid everything—Matthew Winters, memories of the warehouse fire and the dead—only to find all three as soon as he'd come back to Willow Creek. It made his next destination—the secluded Atwood home—all the more enticing.

The second he was through the front door, he decided, he wasn't going to come back out until his next contract. There were no if, ands or buts about it.

Yet, the closer he got to his childhood home, the more his mind went back to the park.

Mack protected the living as a bodyguard; Ray dealt with the dead.

And Willow Creek? It had a past of playing fast and loose with both.

Mack's chest started to grow cold.

That old anger in him wasn't just moving around, it was growing stronger. His grip on the steering wheel turning his knuckles white.

This was why he never stayed in town. No matter what he did, he couldn't escape the past.

Chapter Two

Downtown Willow Creek was divided into two parts. There was the business complex that housed everything law, everything financial and almost everything local politics. This complex, dubbed the Suit Hotel, had desk jockeys who worked in its many rented spaces and were always two things: uptight and dressed ready to kill.

Aiden Riggs took more than a small amount of pleasure walking into his office across the street wearing black joggers and a fitted tee beneath his jean jacket, his Converse high tops still a bit dirty and his hair purposefully styled to look carefree.

Riggs Consulting's lone office worker, Mrs. Cole, however, was less happy with his lack of professional flair. Two seconds through the door and she was already clicking her tongue in disapproval.

"I know I'm no fashionista, but I'm not sure wearing sweats to the office is the way to get more clients."

She pointed to the front display window, and Aiden knew she was motioning to the Suit Hotel. Still, he looked at the window and smiled. Only two of its eighteen tiny panels were transparent; the others were stained to look antique. A charming but failed attempt if you asked Aiden. Still, he'd fallen in love with the window first, the storefront second when he'd first visited the space six months prior. Sure, the office was small, but it was also unique.

It was also as far away from Bellwether Tech's ten-story corporate headquarters in Nashville as you could throw a business.

Right now Mrs. Cole was sitting at her desk in the main lobby; a few feet away was the door to Aiden's office. The two smaller, closet-size rooms next to it were a nook that counted as a break room and then the bathroom, the only two spaces not covered in the clutter that Aiden was so used to accumulating. Much to Mrs. Cole's objections.

Riggs Consulting was nothing like the monster Aiden had left behind.

Even now that thought put him in a good mood.

"Considering we're not hurting for clients, I'd say my clothes don't factor into their decision to hire us." Aiden motioned to his joggers. "In fact, maybe this should be the new professional standard. Are you sure you don't want me to buy you a pair? They're comfortable and, if you need to exercise in a hurry, efficient."

Mrs. Cole, a die-hard fan of pantsuits and floral brooches, narrowed her eyes. The first time Aiden had met her she'd had her hair up in curls and sprayed tight. Since then she'd become more relaxed. At least somewhat. In the words of her husband, she had forty-two years of being a proper Southern lady and a "youngin'" wasn't going to get her guard down that easy. Aiden, in his thirties and not exactly sure he should be considered as such, took the statement as a challenge.

One way or the other he was going to get Mrs. Cole out of her professional shell.

"You can pretend all you want that you don't love me," Aiden said. "But we both know you're my biggest fan."

He sidled up to her desk and put on his brightest smile. Mrs. Cole must have been caught off guard, because the corners of her lips twitched before she rolled her eyes.

"Now, don't you go sweet-talking me and try to make me forget why I'm fussing at you." She took a sticky note from her desktop and handed it over. "Instead go return this call."

Aiden took the paper and read the number in Mrs. Cole's pristine handwriting. He didn't recognize it. The name next to it, however, was an easy memory.

"Leighton called," he read, some surprise mixing in with fondness. "When?"

Mrs. Cole seemed to sense their banter was coming to an end and switched tones to the one she used when working. It wasn't fake, it was just focused.

"At seven thirty this morning," she answered. "I'd just unlocked the front door when the phone started ringing. Mr. Hughes said he might have a job for you but wanted to set up a meeting first."

That caught Aiden's attention even more.

"Did Leighton say if it was urgent?" Aiden checked his watch. It was almost ten in the morning. He'd come in later than usual after pulling an all-nighter for work the day before. You can't catch up on sleep once it's lost, but Aiden sure had tried.

Mrs. Cole shook her head but hesitated. She took her favorite pen in her hand and clicked it open and closed twice. Aiden had seen the same habit come up time and time again when the woman was trying to get her thoughts straight. After a few more clicks, she sighed.

"He said to give him a call at your earliest convenience..."

Aiden's eyebrow rose. She had stopped herself.

"But?"

"But he *sounded* like it was urgent. Like he was being rushed." She clicked the pen again. "I know you need to finish up the last job's paperwork, but I'd go ahead and call him now just in case."

The touch of concern wasn't lost on Aiden. Mrs. Cole wasn't always one who emoted, especially not over a client. Definitely not over a former client who was also Aiden's ex.

"I'll call him as soon as I'm sitting down," Aiden assured her.

Mrs. Cole unclicked her pen top again. When she spoke, there was a maternal warning in her voice.

"And make sure to be on your best behavior when you call," she said. "That's not his personal number, so he might be at work."

Aiden put a gentle hand on her shoulder and squeezed.

"Yes, ma'am. Thanks for the message."

Mrs. Cole returned to the file pulled up on her computer screen, and Aiden took his leave to do just as he'd said.

The space in Riggs Consulting's only office was largely taken up by a wooden desk, an overly padded office chair and a long, narrow table along one wall that housed a bank of computer monitors, all waiting to be used. Aiden dropped his messenger bag on the worn love seat across from the table and went straight for the desk. The chair's wheels squeaked as he situated himself behind it. He couldn't help but compare it and the room around him to the IT department at Bellwether Tech.

If Leighton had called from there, the company's number would have been registered in the caller ID.

Aiden took his cell phone out of his pocket. No missed calls or texts.

If something was urgent, Leighton would have called his cell.

He nodded to himself, trying to dam up his growing sense of worry. They might not have worked out romantically, but Leighton was a good man. Not to mention a client for little things he'd needed help with once or twice since.

Aiden dialed the number on the sticky note and forced himself to lean back in his chair. One thing he loved the most about working in code and on computers? They were a lot more straightforward than the humans who used them.

The line rang a total of six times before an automated voice mail recording picked up. It wasn't personalized. Aiden decided to be as vague.

"This is Aiden Riggs at Riggs Consulting. I'm returning a call from earlier this morning. Feel free to call back anytime." Aiden left his phone number but not Leighton's name. He ended the call.

Something felt off, but he couldn't place what.

"You're overreacting because you've been watching too many thrillers," he said to himself, aloud, after a few moments. "Pull yourself together, Riggs."

Aiden tried to do just that. He dived into the legal paperwork he needed to sign, checked his emails and found a few more tasks that were mind-numbingly boring to pass the time.

But Leighton didn't call back, and by lunch, Aiden couldn't deny he was feeling anxious about it. By noon he was calling Leighton's personal cell phone number. Two hours later he caved and called the last number he'd thought he'd ever dial again.

"Bellwether Technologies, this is the IT department, how may I direct your call?" Aiden felt momentary relief at a somewhat familiar voice.

"Hey, Jenna, it's Aiden. Aiden Riggs."

Jenna Thompson had been the lead executive assistant of the IT department since Aiden had started working there. For six years he'd said hi and bye to Jenna in the morning and afternoon. She'd always been friendly. Even on the day he'd walked out.

"Aiden!" she exclaimed. "Of course I'd know that voice. How are you?"

He shifted in his chair, trying to physically move away from the growing discomfort. Just because he was a social creature didn't mean he always liked being social. Still, it wasn't Jenna's fault that he'd left the company. Acting coldly to her didn't unring the bell of what had happened.

"Hey, I'm good," he responded with tired warmth. "Keeping busy, tanning when I can. Still not eating my vegetables. You know, the usual."

Jenna laughed. The woman definitely had a knack for being peppy.

"You need to get on those veggies, but I'm glad you're doing well otherwise. Though I can't complain too much about your eating habits. You actually just caught me coming back from lunch, and I definitely decided on the bowl of ice cream over the fruit cup."

Aiden joined in on the humor.

Jenna was the first one to drop it.

"What can I do for you?" she asked. "Did you call for me or need a transfer somewhere?"

Aiden could have lied or smooth-talked his way to an excuse that got him some answers without outright asking, but the clenching of his gut that had been tightening since Mrs. Cole gave him Leighton's number wasn't easing. He decided to be blunt, despite the possibility of creating gossip.

"I actually was wondering if Leighton is in the office today?" he decided to go with. "I'd call his extension directly, but I never got the new number."

Silence.

Brief but heavy.

That's when Aiden knew that something really had happened. That Leighton hadn't called just to call.

"Um, I'm not sure," Jenna finally said. "I mean, I don't have that information right now. Could I call you back when I do?"

Aiden sat up a bit straighter.

"You don't know if he's in office today or you don't know his extension?"

She let out a bite of laughter. Nothing about it was genuine.

"Both?" she answered. "It's been a bit chaotic here the last few weeks, and there's been a lot of moving pieces. Let me call you back when I know more. Is this number good?"

On reflex he said it was. Jenna wrapped up the call soon after. She didn't even say bye.

Aiden stared at his phone once it disconnected.

He was still looking at it a few minutes later when Mrs. Cole came in.

"I was finalizing this month's schedule through email when a new one came in just now," she said. "I don't know the sender, but it might be spam."

Aiden took a deep breath and decided to push his worry away. Leighton was an adult. He'd call when he could.

"All right. I'll take a look at it." He took his computer out of sleep mode and pulled up his email inbox. True enough, the latest email was unread.

Mrs. Cole started to leave but paused in the doorway.

"By the way, you're not going to wear that tonight for the party, are you?" She eyed his jacket again with disapproval. For a moment, Aiden had no idea what she was talking about. Then he remembered with a sigh.

"I wouldn't call a grand opening for a coffee shop—at night, mind you—a party."

Mrs. Cole rolled her eyes.

"I don't care what you consider it. All the downtown business owners are going to be there—we're going, too." She pointed at him with purpose. "So make sure you go home early and get some clothes that have buttons and zippers, not drawstrings. Understood?"

Some employers might have taken the command as offensive, but Aiden knew that Mrs. Cole cared about him. That was enough to make him agree.

"Yes, ma'am," he conceded. "Buttons, not strings."

Mrs. Cole gave him a quick nod of approval and shut the door behind her. Aiden's smile fell away in the time between. Then he was staring at the opened email on his computer screen.

The sender's email address was omitted.

The subject line was only one exclamation mark.

There was no signature line or any mention of the sender's name.

But, despite having no proof, Aiden couldn't help but

believe that the text in the body of the email had been written by Leighton Hughes.

If I die, Bellwether Tech killed me.

Chapter Three

Mack was never one to indulge in napping, but after he returned to the Atwood homestead and unpacked, his entire body decided to drag him down against his will. He went from alert and thoughtful to belly up in his childhood bedroom, the air conditioner blowing white noise and cold around him while the rest of the house didn't make a peep. Maybe it was that silence that really did the trick. When he opened his eyes again, the sunlight through the curtain had changed positions.

The house had also collected a few new sounds.

Mack stared at the ceiling as he heard the footsteps echoing from the other side of the house.

Someone was in the kitchen. Making coffee? Making lunch?

He didn't bother looking at his phone to see how long he'd been asleep. When he was working a contract, he budgeted every minute of his time. When he was at home in between? He didn't mind getting lost in the seconds.

The noise in the kitchen continued, though, and Mack knew it didn't matter if he wanted to stay right where he was for the rest of the day and night. He might not be on a contract, but he'd have someone to answer to soon.

He sighed into the old room and got up slowly. The

bandage beneath his shirt caught and pulled a little, but he ignored the annoyance. Like the over-the-top greeting he was sure to get in the near future, there wasn't anything he could do to make the ache he'd gotten in the past disappear. He'd done everything right and still gotten a knife for his trouble. There was no point complaining about it now.

Mack left the bedroom with another heavy sigh.

Sometimes he couldn't believe the same halls he'd walked as a kid, he was walking as an adult. After all these years, after everything that happened outside its walls, here he was rattling around the same two-story house he'd learned to walk in. Life sure was interesting sometimes.

The same familiar path from his bedroom at the back end of the first floor to the kitchen spanned almost the length of the house. With his long legs, Mack's stride had him at the kitchen sink and staring at Finn within a few blinks.

Running into his little brother first was the most ideal situation he could have hoped for after coming home.

Finn, twenty-six but still as bright-eyed and smiling as he'd been as a little kid, greeted Mack with an outstretched hand holding a mug.

"I figured you'd rise and shine the second I made my afternoon coffee," Finn said. "Sorry if I woke you up, though. You must be tired after your early flight."

Mack took the mug and shrugged off the apology.

"You know I've never been one to sleep that long," he said. "I'm surprised I got the shut-eye I did. What time is it, exactly?"

Finn went to grab another mug from the cabinet. He was grinning.

"Must have been a good nap if you have no idea how long you were asleep. It's almost one."

Mack nodded. Not bad for a nap.

He took a seat at the eat-in kitchen table and stretched his legs out long.

Finn wasn't as tall as him, but he'd always made up any physical gaps between them with a cleverness and quickness that had often surprised, and annoyed, Mack growing up. Whereas he had the muscles and power, Finn had the talking down pat. He was the charmer of the family, the one who could outtalk anyone if given the opportunity. It made him a dangerous salesperson, which was why he'd become the only in-house medical sales representative at the hospital two years prior.

Finick Atwood was the second most popular Atwood still living in Willow Creek.

The first?

Well, Mack hoped to avoid her a little longer.

Something that Finn must have picked up on.

"I'd say you have a few minutes to drink that coffee before hell on wheels comes in," Finn said, a light laugh ending his words.

Mack snorted.

"Is that your twin radar warning you?" he asked.

Finn made a so-so gesture with his hand.

"That and the fact she called a few minutes ago."

His little brother gave him a quick look, but it said enough for Mack. Word about the John Doe at the park had already gotten out. Word about him being there, too, if he had to guess.

Mack took a long pull of his coffee. When he was done, he decided one more long sigh would do. Finn leaned against the counter by the window. He was keeping watch, but he wasn't going to ask anything until the third of their trio made it in. Instead, Finn did what he did best.

He found something else to talk about.

"A new coffee shop opened up downtown since the last time you were here," he started. "They're having a grand opening party tonight, and we've all been invited."

Mack knew where this was going.

"I'm going to go ahead and decline that invite," he said, sure to show his conviction. "I'd rather stay here and drink this stuff." He shook his mug. Finn snorted.

"You can talk big and bad all you want, but there's no point in fooling ourselves." He glanced out the window. A smile, more mischievous than it should have been, pulled up the corners of his lips. "We both know Mother Hen isn't going to let you skip a big social event while you're in town. And, if you don't believe me, then let's wait about thirty seconds."

Mack heard the gravel crunching and, like he knew where the conversation would lead with his brother, he knew that their mother hen had finally returned to the hen house.

"All right," Mack said, standing tall. "Let's get this over with."

The Atwood homestead stretched wide and dipped here and there for a good few acres of land. There were trees around every corner, a creek that ran around one edge of the property and a freestanding but vacated barn on the back half, a building none of them could consider getting rid of since their great-granddaddy had built it. Between the Atwood siblings, each had their own little favorite spot of the land for their own reasons. Mack's just happened to be the easiest to see.

Across the drive that led from the main road up to the house was a field. There was nothing special about it, and it held no function. It was simply an expanse of grass with no trees or flowers or fences. An open space with nothing to offer the world except the promise that, if you stood in its middle, there wasn't a thing that would touch you.

And that's why Mack liked it so much.

Just looking across the drive, not looking too far off at the trees, you'd find a bunch of empty.

There was a beauty in that, and it was a beauty that he often thought about when he was away from home.

Even now, over the wild blond hair of the woman hurrying out of her beat-up Bronco in between Mack and the field, he felt his chest loosen. His breathing calmed. His shoulders relaxed.

The empty comforted him.

Which was a good thing considering his sister was about to fill him up with her own worries.

"I told you to go straight home when you flew in and instead you go to a dang *murder* scene?"

Marigold Atwood was the youngest Atwood by mere minutes, but out of the three of them, she reigned queen. Since even before their father passed and their mother left, Goldie had been the one behind the scenes trying to make the best of their lives. From school to career to friendships and romance, she had her hands in all the Atwood pies. It had driven her twin, Finn, up the wall when they were teens, but now, in their late twenties, he'd accepted the fact that their sister had taken over the role of matriarch. It was easier to listen to what she had to say rather than avoid it. Mack being older than her had no bearing on that fact.

He tucked his chin a little and smiled a little more.

"Hey there, Goldie," he said. "I missed you, too."

Goldie wasn't as enthused. All five-nine of her stopped at the bottom step of the front porch and glared up at him.

"Give me one reason why I shouldn't smack some kind of sense into you, Malcolm Gene Atwood," she said, ignoring his greeting.

Finn moved to Mack's side and sucked on his teeth.

"Oh, man, she three-named you," he whispered. "Rest in pieces there, brother."

Mack dropped his smile and held up his hands in defense.

"It was a quick detour and didn't require any heavy lifting," he explained. "All I did was go and look at something and then got my tail here and in bed for some rest. No harm, no foul."

Finn nodded.

"That's the truth right there," he confirmed. "I'm witness to the fact that he just got up from a nap."

Mama Goldie wasn't in the mood for their tag teaming. Her hands went to her hips and that glare became near slits.

"From what I heard you didn't just go and look at nothing. You went and looked at a dead body. Heavy lifting or not, your mind needs just as much rest as your body after a long contract." Goldie glanced down at his chest. "Especially after a job you bled for."

Her glare softened.

Any annoyance Mack had for his sister fizzled out, too.

Ray had said it once before.

"I've never met someone so loud at loving."

That was Goldie, all right. She didn't filter her worries or anger or happiness when it came to her loved ones. She said what was on her mind, and she said it with absolute devotion.

That's why Mack held back the urge to defend himself, his injury and his choice to go see Ray and John Doe.

Goldie was just caring loudly at him. It would be rude to try and make her feel bad about that.

Mack lowered his head until his chin was almost touching his chest. He kept eye contact but hoped he looked apologetic enough.

"I'm sorry," he said. "I should have been more thoughtful to myself. I also should have called. Sorry, sis."

A silence squeezed its way between his apology and her frustration. Finn was the first person to take advantage of it with his powers of persuasion.

"Make him show how sorry he is by getting him to come with us tonight to the grand-opening hoopla," he said. "He already thinks he isn't going to go."

Mack went from apologetic to trying to play wounded real quick.

"She just said I need to mind my health by resting. I don't think partying is what the doctor would order."

Both brothers turned back to Goldie. Mack should have known he was going to lose by the way Finn was already smiling. He for sure knew he was done when Goldie mimicked her twin's expression.

"I've never met a man who would take a knife to his body without blinking but will come up with excuses to avoid being social." She reached up and patted his shoulder. "If you can stand and brood at a crime scene, you can stand and brood in a coffee shop."

Mack opened his mouth to argue, but Goldie was already

walking past him. The words she threw over her shoulder sealed his fate.

"And you're going to wear a suit while doing it, too."

Finn laughed, Mack sighed and Goldie could be heard chuckling as she went inside the house.

He didn't miss much about Willow Creek, not since the fire. Not since everyone forgot about his father. Mack, though, felt like he was slipping as close into comfort as he could when he was with the twins.

It was a feeling that stayed for a while as he kept his spot on the front porch. He stared out at the empty field and let his thoughts crowd it a little. Finn wasn't surprised at the fact that he'd been at a homicide that morning. Goldie hadn't asked a single question about it or John Doe. She also hadn't asked to see his wound, just as Finn hadn't, either.

"They're giving me space," Mack whispered to himself. He kept staring at the field. He knew it was the last empty he'd be getting for a while, especially if he was being forced to attend a party downtown. Mack had never been Mr. Popular in school, but his job certainly earned him a lot of questions whenever he was out and about in town. Goldie and Finn's natural charisma wasn't going to help matters, either. He could already picture both being pulled away to chat about something while he was left standing in the corner with his drink, watching the clock.

Mack gave the field another long look and slipped past his family to go back to his room. He scooped up his cell phone and clicked on Ray's number.

The call rang several times before his friend answered. "Hello?"

Mack bypassed a normal greeting. He went straight for the bottom line.

"You owe me, so pay me back by standing with me at a party tonight. I can't take no for an answer, so don't try and come up with an excuse."

What was better than being forced to withstand a social event you didn't want to go to? Forcing someone to attend it with you.

However, to his surprise, Ray didn't come back with the sarcastic retort Mack would have expected.

"Let me call you back," he said instead. "I have someone here."

Mack tilted his head to the side. He couldn't help but be curious.

"Does that mean someone identified John Doe?"

Ray didn't answer for a moment. When he did his voice had lowered.

"It's gotten complicated," he said. "Let me call you later."

The line went dead before Mack could respond.

Complicated.

Mack's hands balled into fists. The memory of smoke filling his nostrils and pain filling his heart burned through him. The last time Mack had heard that word in Willow Creek his entire life had changed.

He refused to give Willow Creek that power again.

Chapter Four

Aiden walked into the party, and all he saw were lines of code. Thirty or so, with tags that read dressed-up in nice suits and dresses, shiny shoes and carefully styled hair, and each with one fundamental task to execute.

Mingle.

"I know you've had a day and a half, but try to enjoy yourself," Mrs. Cole said at his side. She brought him a drink from the coffee bar that was currently housing an assortment of bottles, cans, cups and finger foods. He could smell a little alcohol in it. This was the first time Mrs. Cole had offered such a drink to him. Aiden thought he might should mark the day. There was no need, though. Mrs. Cole had been hovering since they'd gone to the hospital together a few hours earlier.

Gossip had broken the sound barrier in Willow Creek and brought the terrifying news that a man had been found murdered in the park. After that, he'd gone to the morgue with Mrs. Cole knowing in his heart of hearts that Leighton Hughes had in fact met his end.

Yet, the medical examiner hadn't even let Aiden through the door.

"You said your friend has dark hair, dark skin and a

scar along his forearm. Our John Doe doesn't have any of the three."

The fist of relief that had punched into Aiden's chest had been one heck of a wallop.

That feeling didn't wholly stay.

Partially thanks to a man Aiden had instantly disliked walking up into their conversation with a particularly judgmental air about him.

"Word gets out about a homicide and you're the first to bust tail to get here to see if your buddy is the one we're trying to identify," he'd said. "Not many people's gut tells them to go check the morgue when someone is missing less than a day."

The man had shown his badge then.

Detective Winters, the sheriff department's ace.

A self-imposed description that had gotten an almost eye roll out of the medical examiner still standing at their sides. Aiden had watched the two stare at one another with what he could only interpret as genuine dislike until the detective had suggested they go to the department to talk. Mrs. Cole was the only reason he readily agreed. That and, well, he couldn't get it out of his head that even though John Doe wasn't Leighton, his friend was still in trouble.

A feeling that had pricked up an even older, familiar feeling he'd promised himself he'd never indulge again.

Mrs. Cole, who still didn't know the extent of how different he'd been before coming to Willow Creek, did a good job of helping him avoid falling back into that pit. Even without realizing it.

"You need to get out and socialize," she'd said. "If eating good food with good people isn't enough of a reason to get your mind clear for a while, then look at it as an opportunity to soak in the gossip. Who knows, you might find something interesting floating among the loose-lipped."

And that's what had gotten Aiden to the main room of Sue and Mae's Café.

He was looking at something he fully understood.

Lines of code, entry points for potential information.

Scripts being written, waiting for him to get the digital download.

If there was a link between Leighton and John Doe, maybe he'd find it here.

It was a long shot, but he'd take it.

He accepted the drink from Mrs. Cole and lowered his voice.

"Who has the loosest but most reliable lips here?"

On any other day, Mrs. Cole might have ignored the question, but she'd been overly warm to him since John Doe had entered their picture. It was touching. It was also useful. She scanned the guests in the main dining room and then nodded toward the wall opposite them.

"Patty Truit, the woman with the hair sprayed high over there, usually knows what people are doing in this town before those people even know they're doing it," she said.

Patty looked familiar. Mrs. Cole picked up on the re-alization.

"She brought in a fruit basket the first week after you opened. You don't come into town without an official in-person meet and greet from Patty."

"Then she's the one I need to talk to," Aiden decided.

"If you're looking for stray news, then she's definitely the one to hover around," she agreed. Aiden nodded and was about to set out to see exactly how useful that line of code was, but Mrs. Cole caught him by the elbow.

"But, first, we're going to be polite and say hello to our hosts. Nice smile, Mr. Riggs. Make those buttons you're wearing shine."

Sue and Mae's Café was cute and surprisingly spacious. Housed in a stand-alone building across the street from Riggs Consulting, its perfectly square shape allowed for a large dining room with a long coffee bar and display case, walls covered in rustic decorations and enough floor space to fit the thirty or so guests comfortably.

Aiden followed Mrs. Cole into the thick of well-dressed people and right to the owners and said their greetings. Mae, the mother of the mother-daughter duo, was nice. Aiden had met her in passing before, and together they said all the polite, proper things. Sue, he guessed in her early twenties, wasn't as reserved. When Mrs. Cole and Mae were swept into another conversation deeper in the heart of the dining room, Sue's eyes became alight with enthusiasm.

"You used to live in Nashville, right?"

Aiden couldn't help but reflect the smile.

"I did," he confirmed. "For almost ten years."

Sue did a little dance with her feet.

"I love Nashville, like, truly love it," she said. "I went for a competition there a few years ago and had an absolute blast. We stayed at this hotel-resort thing that had like a city inside it. It was so cool and pretty."

"Ah." Aiden knew what she was talking about. He laughed. "That would be the Opryland Resort. It's very popular. I've gone there before, but it was for a conference. I've never had a chance to stay in one of their rooms, though."

That only made Sue all the more bouncy.

"Oh, it was a blast! Me and a few other competitors got

lost *inside* on the first night. I've never almost gotten lost in a hotel before."

Aiden raised an eyebrow at the "competitors" part.

"What kind of competition was it? I know they hold all kinds."

Aiden had never met Sue before, but at that he could tell she realized she'd said too much. Her cheeks tinted red, and her smile wavered. She still answered, but there was a nervous trill of laughter attached to it.

"It was a computer thing. Not a big deal."

"Computer things are my bread and butter!" He waved her modesty off. "And usually competitions involving computers are no joke. Was it a coding thing? Software or hardware?"

She seemed worried that he might not like her answer.

Aiden decided then to change topics. However, a newcomer slid into their conversation with his own answers.

"Don't let Sue here sell herself short," he started. "You're looking at Willow Creek's very own video game queen right here. She placed in the top ten of the country, bringing honor and bragging rights to us all."

He was a good-looking man in a suit, closer to Sue's age and smiling as brightly as she had been a minute before. Aiden watched as the two seemed to be trying to have a conversation between their gazes and Sue's cheeks went to a shade almost as red as a stop sign.

Aiden didn't understand the embarrassment.

"What?" he said. "That's amazing. Video game competitions are fierce, not to mention the skill and focus it takes to actually place in them. If I were you, I'd wear that around on my shirt every day."

"Right?" the man exclaimed at his side. "See, Sue! I told you. You should be proud."

Sue didn't seem convinced. She smiled into a sigh then forced a laugh.

"It's in the past now." She motioned to the room around them. "This is my new focus with Mom."

The man shook his head. He gave Aiden a look that said they'd had a conversation like this before.

"I told her she should do both. Maybe even carve out a gaming, internet café-type corner in here." This time he sighed, but there was no real weight to it. "But who am I to force Sue Walding to do anything? Greatness should be able to make its own decisions, after all."

Aiden watched the man's words pull Sue's earlier smile back out to bloom again. He wondered what kind of relationship the two had.

"Speaking of greatness." Sue stretched out her hand and moved it between the two of them. "I don't know if you've met yet, Aiden, but, this is one of Willow Creek's favorite people, Finn Atwood. Finn, this is Aiden Riggs."

Finn shook Aiden's hand with vigor and laughed at the introduction.

"We all know there's only one true favorite Atwood here in town, but it's good to know Sue Walding thinks so highly of me." Finn looked to Aiden. "So you're Riggs of Riggs Consulting, right?"

Aiden nodded.

"That's me."

"I bet you're getting some good business here," Finn said. "I'm not putting down our town but I know a lot of our residents aren't that tech or internet savvy. My brother alone could keep you in business year-round."

Aiden opened his mouth to respond, but Sue popped up again like a flower angling for the sun.

"Speaking of your brother, I heard he came back to town this morning." She lowered her voice. "And got caught up in the trouble at the park."

Aiden's ears perked at that.

While he didn't know who John Doe was, Aiden did know he'd been found at the park. Was Finn's brother law enforcement?

His smile became tight, but he didn't seem offended by the question. Instead he lowered his voice to match Sue's volume.

"He was asked for a favor, but he didn't stay long."

Sue did something weird. She motioned to her face but didn't say anything.

Yet Finn nodded like she'd asked a question.

"He's here tonight, so if you want to know more you should talk to him. But, well, you know him. He'll find a way to escape soon, so I suggest you do it sooner rather than later." Finn turned to survey the room. He stopped and nodded toward a group by the front door. "There he is, already making eyes at the back door."

Aiden followed his line of sight out of curiosity.

He knew of the Atwoods only in passing. They lived on the largest piece of residential land in the county but weren't exactly rich. When people spoke of them, it had been pleasant enough. If any gossip had circulated about them, Aiden had missed it. He hadn't even known who made up the family behind the name, let alone that the Atwoods were popular enough to earn the title of town favorites.

But, when Aiden's eyes stopped on the spot where Finn was looking, he understood the Atwood allure.

Standing just inside the front doorway was a man who

might as well have been a neon light in a dark, empty room. He was tall, a tree that reached for the sky with shoulders broad enough to hold it. His hair was neat and dark and made his tan seem more golden than not. His facial features were sharp, there was no stubble or five o'clock anything to detract from the near crispness, and from across the room Aiden could see that even his eyes had an awe to them. They matched his brother's blue. However, unlike Finn's brand of nice looks, his brother wrapped in a suit felt different.

You noticed him, though. The way he stood gave Aiden the impression that he might not be a man who wanted to be noticed.

It was a powerful look.

One that intrigued Aiden to no end, especially when that brother caught their collective gaze on him.

Finn said, "Busted."

Sue laughed a little.

Aiden didn't move a muscle.

The man's attention went wholly to him.

If Aiden's phone hadn't vibrated deep in his pocket, he might have just stood there and kept staring. Gotten a little lost. Instead he broke eye contact and pulled his phone out.

It was an unknown caller.

Maybe it was Leighton?

"Excuse me, I need to take this."

Aiden's mind left the man at the door altogether.

He didn't have time to wonder why the man was still staring at him as he walked by.

ALL MACK SAW when he walked into the party were faces. Ones that were, and had been, in his memory database for years. Locals, schoolmates, friends of the twins. The people who'd made up Willow Creek since he was a kid. Sure, he knew he hadn't seen some of them in a long while, but regardless, their faces would be in his memory, ready for him.

But then something happened.

Mack saw a face he didn't recognize.

The man wasn't nearly as tall as him, but somehow he managed to stand out among the guests. Maybe it was because his appearance itself wasn't what Mack was used to in Willow Creek. He was wearing all black, yet it was like he'd been highlighted among the sea of outfits around him. His hair was light and slicked back, showing a piercing at the top of one ear, and there was a relaxed sway to his stance despite the fact that he wasn't moving. Compared to the many faces that Mack had floating in his memory, this man had no odd or special attributes to him. No mass of freckles, no scars, no moles or birthmarks. Angled and sharp features, sure, but nothing that should have set him apart from others.

Yet Mack couldn't look away from the green eyes that had locked with his.

Not even as the man walked out of the party.

Then, to confuse himself even further, Mack joined his brother with a question instead of a greeting.

"Who was that?"

Finn smirked.

"Ah, I'm guessing it's weird for you to see someone for the first time." He pointed to the front display windows. "You know the consulting business I told you about across the street? The one that deals with IT-y things? He's the owner."

"Aiden Riggs," Sue supplied politely.

Mack nodded to her, since he'd glossed over a hello. Among Finn's friends, he liked Sue the most. She'd never peppered him with questions.

"He's been here about six months," she added.

Finn clapped Mack on the shoulder.

"And, like you, he seems to be a bit antisocial," he said. "This is the first time I've seen him."

Mack glanced out the display windows. He couldn't see the man anymore.

Not that it should matter.

His interest was just the novelty of seeing someone new, he decided.

And that's the thought he kept with him as the minutes went by and Aiden Riggs didn't return. Mack continued to dismiss his attention on the man's absence as those minutes rolled into a half hour. Fifteen minutes after that, Mack decided he just needed to get his curiosity out.

So he googled the man's name.

Aiden Riggs had several search results.

His business was the first, his social media was the second and the third was a pinned review from a happy client.

The fourth, however, pulled Mack in.

It was an article with a picture preview. A tech company had won a bid, and among those who worked there was a group celebrating while wearing party hats and smiling wide at the camera.

Mack's eye was drawn to Aiden first.

Then his gaze swept over to someone else in the picture. Someone he recognized.

Mack froze in place.

Standing behind Aiden in the picture was a man with freckles all over his face.

A man Mack had seen that morning.

John Doe.

Chapter Five

The party across the street must have been wrapping up. When Aiden locked Riggs Consulting's front door, the night was oddly quiet. It probably didn't help that he'd spent over an hour in his office getting lost in his own little world. Not even Mrs. Cole's call of disapproval had brought him back to the festivities.

Aiden had had tunnel vision, and exiting said tunnel had become surprisingly difficult.

The unknown number that had called him at the party had stayed unknown.

No one had been on the other end of the line when he'd answered the phone, just some static and an eventual dial tone when the call ended. It had driven Aiden up the wall, especially after he'd called back and gotten a standard voice mail recording.

He'd stared at his phone for a bit after that, wondering if his anxiety was mounting for nothing. Maybe he was bored and Leighton, John Doe and the email about Bell-wether Tech were just excuses for him to feel some kind of excitement. Maybe he was lonely. His only companions in Willow Creek were Mrs. Cole and her husband. Even then, it wasn't like he spent many after-work hours with them.

Maybe he was borrowing trouble just to feel *more*.

Aiden had shaken that idea off as soon as it had slid in. Still, though, he remained behind his desk. After that his attention had wandered back to the email about Bellwether Tech.

If I die, Bellwether Tech killed me.

Aiden didn't understand why the message hadn't had a name attached. If you wanted to report on your potential murder, then wouldn't you want to say who you were?

It made no sense.

None of it made sense.

That's when Aiden had finally had enough.

Just because there wasn't a name in the email signature didn't mean he couldn't find out who had sent it. Or, rather, where it was sent from.

"If you start peeking behind the curtain, you might not stop," Aiden had told himself before fully committing to his new idea. "This whole thing probably isn't a big deal. You're just nosy."

He'd stared at his computer for a while longer.

The last time he'd used a computer to snoop, he'd inadvertently changed the course of his future. All it had taken were a few keystrokes and clicks.

Did he want to do that again just to figure out where the email came from?

Was it that big of a deal?

What if the email was a joke? A bad one but a joke all the same?

Was it worth toeing the line between what he should do in his professional life and what he shouldn't do in his personal life?

Aiden had wasted most of his time in the office debating this question.

Then he'd caved.

While he was skilled in the IT field and did well enough on the hardware side of it, Aiden absolutely thrived at one specific thing.

He was an excellent hacker.

His fingers had flown across the keyboard like a warm knife slicing through butter. The mouse had felt like it was an extension of his hand, his fingers moving to a rhythm that didn't skip a beat. He found the anonymous email sender's location in under two minutes. During that time he'd even double-checked the name.

The urge to go further had nearly done him in.

Instead he'd pushed himself out of Riggs Consulting and now was deep within the night air.

"The email was sent from Willow Creek," he told the door, talking to himself to process the information. When he put the office key in his pocket, he exchanged it for the sticky note he'd written the sender's address on. "It has to be from Leighton, right?"

Why else would Bellwether find its way to him *from* a local address?

There was only one way to find out.

Aiden nodded to himself and thrust his hand and the note back into his blazer's pocket. He followed the sidewalk around the building to the parking lot that stretched behind Riggs Consulting. It only had two narrow rows of spaces and one lone streetlamp positioned between the asphalt and the wooded area enclosing the lot. Some parking spots were in rough condition and no one dared park in them. Others were for employees of neighboring buildings. After work hours, it wasn't unusual for Aiden's silver hatchback to be sitting solo in the lot.

That's why he had no thought to check that he was, in fact, alone.

He got into the front seat of his car and shut the door behind him. His laptop bag went on the passenger's seat; his phone went into one of the cupholders. As he'd done countless times before, he slid the key into the ignition with one hand and put his seat belt on with the other.

It was by pure chance that he saw the reflection of the man in the back seat in the rearview mirror.

Aiden didn't even have time to yell before an arm snaked around his headrest. The move pinned his neck against the seat with a viselike grip that was as strong as it was terrifying. His breath went out; his adrenaline soared. His hands went up next, trying to pry himself free.

It didn't work.

Aiden's fingers wrapped under the man's arm, but the grip remained tight. He tried to beat the arm next but none of his movements seemed to have an effect on his attacker.

That's when he tried to outthink his panic.

Wasn't there an easy way to get out of a hold like this?

He'd seen a viral instructional video about it before, but what was he supposed to do now?

Aiden swiped back behind him, hoping to land a hit. Instead he touched fabric, and even that he couldn't get a hold on. It was like the man had managed to find the one position that had utterly and completely made him defenseless.

So Aiden decided to make some noise.

He laid on the steering wheel, and the horn started to blare.

The grip around his neck tightened. Aiden swiped back

again with one hand and tried to pry him off with the other. His head was starting to pound; his lungs were burning. His vision was starting to be affected. Something was moving out of the corner of his eye with startling speed. He wondered if he was about to lose consciousness.

Then he thought he had.

Night air rushed into the car.

But not next to him.

A loud grunt sounded as the grip around Aiden's neck loosened.

A second later it disappeared altogether.

Aiden leaned forward, coughing and sputtering and trying to get the oxygen he'd been deprived of. He only managed to see what was happening because the action had changed locations.

Instead of the man choking him from behind, he was no longer in the car at all.

He was standing next to it, the back door wide-open.

And he wasn't alone.

THE MAN WAS BIG, but Mack was bigger.

When he grabbed him and yanked him out of the car, the man came out in one fluid movement. That might have been partially due to the surprise of Mack's sudden intervention, though. Mack followed the arc of his momentum and slung the guy farther away from the car. There wasn't even a peep out of him. Never mind a fight-or-flight response to the new danger.

That wouldn't last long.

Mack watched as the man caught himself before hitting the ground. He stumbled but he recovered quickly.

He was athletic, Mack figured.

He was also covered head to toe.

A dark blue hoodie was pulled tight over his head, covering his hair. He had on dark jeans and black tennis shoes, while his hands were wrapped in gloves and, from his nose down, his face was covered in a black gaiter. Mack could only see a sliver of a pale face and dark brown eyes.

Eyes that seemed to size him up with speed.

And make a decision even quicker.

Mack shifted his right foot back a little and tightened his stance just as the man lunged toward him. Instead of throwing a punch, the man swiped at Mack's blazer.

He was a grabber, Mack's least favorite type of fighter. A clinger whose whole strategy was to push or pull their opponent off balance to try and get the advantage.

Mack had met many a grabber before. He'd lost to one on his first-ever private security job. He'd been slung to the ground and then kicked over and over again before getting back the upper hand. Since then he had never lost to a grabber.

So he wasn't going to start now.

Mack caught the man's outstretched wrist with his left hand and then threw a punch straight to his nose with his right. Since he had the man in his grasp, he couldn't escape the hit.

The man recoiled with a yell. Mack had either busted his nose or broken it. If it wasn't for the mask, he was sure he'd see blood.

"Stop fighting," Mack warned his opponent. He'd lost his grip after the punch, but the man was holding his face and hunched over no more than a few steps away now. Mack could have kept volleying, but there was no point in forcing the man down when he was already going there himself.

Just in case he wasn't aware of his odds, Mack spelled it out for him. "You can either talk with me or have me come at you again. Your choice."

Mack heard the car door open behind him. Shoes crunched the asphalt as Aiden must have stepped out.

Which meant he was okay.

A feeling of relief washed over Mack.

He pushed it away to focus on the hooded figure.

His eyes cut over Mack's shoulder. They narrowed.

Then the man turned tail and ran.

Mack wasn't going to let that one go.

"Call the cops," he yelled over his shoulder. Then he was boots to the asphalt.

The man might not have been an ace fighter, but when it came to running he was a rabbit after a carrot. He streaked across the parking lot before cutting left into the wooded area at its back. Mack knew Willow Creek inside and out. Just like he knew they would be forced to slow down to navigate the dense trees, he knew that on the other side of them was the back of Dillard's Grocery Store, followed by Second Street. If the sheriff's department dispatched from their headquarters over near the county line, then they would drive in on the other side of downtown. Which meant if Mack didn't catch the man soon, he stood a good chance of using Second Street to get away before backup came.

That possibility didn't sit right with him.

Mack leaned into his run and split between the trees. This patch of trees in Willow Creek was one of several wooded areas downtown. It didn't stretch as wide as some of the others, but it was enough to slow both Mack and the man down. A branch he couldn't see clipped Mack's shoulder a yard or so in. Then he heard the man ahead of him yell out as he must have also hit something. It didn't help that visibility was almost nonexistent. The possibility that he might actually lose him started to rise until a light in the distance became a beacon. The man was heading toward it, too. Mack watched his outline hustle in the direction before disappearing.

Mack burst out of the trees and skidded across the back alley of the grocery store. His legs were burning and his side had some sting to it, but his focus was narrowing back. He tilted his head to the side and listened.

Footsteps echoed to his right.

He took off again.

Sirens sounded in the distance. Maybe there was a cruiser that was closer than he thought.

Mack ran the length of the grocery store's building and rounded the corner.

He skidded to a halt.

The knife sliced through the night air and narrowly missed his arm.

He windmilled backward. It made him lose his footing in the process. Pain lit up his side as Mack connected with the paved path.

The man didn't waste the opening.

He followed Mack to the ground, arcing the knife downward.

There was no space or time to fully dodge or fully attack, so Mack did a little of both. He threw his arm up to cover the space above his head and kicked out. The man let out a yell as Mack's foot connected with his ankle.

But he didn't fall.

Instead he brought his knife back in an arc, this time with more power behind it.

Mack was going to have to take it. There was nothing else he could do. He just hoped to take it in the hand or arm, not the side or face. If the damage wasn't too severe, he could deal with the pain after he got the weapon away.

It was his only option.

The man was surprisingly fast.

Mack saw the blade of the knife coming down. He braced himself.

Then watched in confusion as the man went from standing to on the ground next to him, limp. The knife clattered to the pavement. Mack blinked several times.

That's when he realized a third person had entered their fight.

Standing behind where the man had been was none other than Aiden Riggs.

He had a wooden baseball bat in his hands.

He went from looking at the now-unconscious man to Mack. His eyes were wide, but his voice was steady. His first words to Mack were as out of pocket as his sudden appearance and save.

"Is it bad I want to call my Little League coach right now?"

Mack stared.

"What?"

Aiden shook the bat.

"He told me I couldn't hit the broad side of a barn even if I was standing next to it. Looks like my aim got way better, huh?"

Mack heard the nerves in Aiden's voice, the adrenaline no doubt still surging, and knew it was no small thing to hurt a person even in the defense of others.

Yet, in that moment, he did something that surprised him.

He laughed.

Chapter Six

The La Forge County Sheriff's Department was an uneven building resting across a raised hill and a flat piece of land. No one quite understood why they hadn't built the structure solely on the latter, since they'd had to accommodate for the weirdness by splitting their building in two. On the right, hill side of the building were the lobby and offices. On the left, flat side sat the cells and interrogation rooms meant for the detained.

Aiden was in a meeting room on the right side, glad he wasn't having to visit the other. He wasn't one to shy away from the ill-intentioned but he didn't think being in close proximity to the man he had beaten down with his Little League baseball bat was the best idea. A sentiment his Atwood friend had seemed to share. Once some deputies had found them behind the grocery store and asked them to come to the department and provide statements, he'd been loud in requesting they wait somewhere near the lobby but out of sight. So that's where they were, tucked away in a meeting room near the lobby, just the two of them.

And that's where Aiden had been trying his best not to let his mouth run off while staring at his temporary partner in crime.

Mack. Atwood.

Tall, dark, handsome and apparently not very talkative.

It had been making Aiden restless since they had settled into their chairs. One of them was fine with the silence. The other? Not so much.

Finally, as that other, Aiden broke.

"I know I already said it, but thank you again for helping me out." He rolled his chair up to the table a little more, hoping if he got closer to the man, he would be more inclined to be chatty.

Mack, however, wasn't fazed by the move. Sitting opposite Aiden like he was going to lead some kind of interview, he kept looking at his phone.

Aiden cleared his throat.

"I used to think people who check the back seats of their cars were being paranoid," he continued. "But now I don't think I'll ever not do that when getting into one. I still can't believe he was there. I also can't believe you showed up."

That part got a reaction, though not Mack's gaze.

"I was leaving Sue and Mae's party and heard you blowing the horn," he said matter-of-factly. "After that I just tried to help like anyone else would have."

Aiden was slightly suspicious now, as he had been earlier when he had tried to run the math in his head. It felt like Mack had shown up way too fast after Aiden had hit the horn, especially if he had been leaving the café across the street. Maybe that was another Mack Atwood power, super speed.

Then again, Aiden hadn't exactly been in the right mind to keep an accurate time count going.

His throat still hurt now as he spoke.

He pretended it didn't.

"Either way, I'm lucky you did," he said. "I guess I'm also

lucky that I bring that bat everywhere with me. I've never had to handle someone wielding a knife like they were in some kind of action movie before."

Mack's eyes went up at that.

This was the closest Aiden had been to the man where he could see him in clear lighting. His eyes weren't just blue. They were the sea.

"You shouldn't have had to test your luck at all. I don't know what you were doing before you came to Willow Creek, but it's not a smart move to run after someone who nearly killed you."

Mack's words had a bite to them. Aiden didn't appreciate them or it.

"You saved me, and then I tried to save you," he returned. "I don't know how that's a bad thing. Especially since you were the only one without a weapon. If anything, *you* shouldn't have run after him."

The big guy wasn't a fan of that response.

He dropped his phone and crossed his arms over his chest.

"I was handling myself just fine, thanks."

Aiden mirrored his posture.

"The way I saw it, you were about to take a knife to the arm had I not stepped in."

The man snorted.

"Just because it looked that way doesn't mean I didn't have it handled," Mack grumbled. "I encounter things like this all the time in my profession."

"Almost getting stabbed?" Aiden leaned forward. "Or thumbing your nose at people who obviously helped you?"

Mack looked like he was ready to say something even more biting but stopped himself as the door to the room opened. Aiden's mood had already fallen, yet it managed to drop a few more notches as he recognized the new addition.

Detective Winters was dressed down in a collared shirt and jeans. He still had his badge on display, hanging around his neck. He adjusted it as he addressed Mack first.

"Well, if it isn't the prodigal son returned to town."

The tone was friendly, but the smirk that followed didn't match.

Aiden looked between the two men. The annoyance that had been there a few seconds ago had hardened into something a lot more meaningful. Aiden might not have known the Atwood man, but with one glance at how he was staring at the detective, there was no doubt that Mack didn't like him.

Not at all.

His jaw was clenched, his shoulders were tight and his voice had dropped into a smooth detachment.

"I'm not here long," was all he said.

The detective seemed bemused by the answer. He took a seat at the head of the table and leaned back in his chair.

"Well, it's good to hear business is booming. With the way that brother of yours talks about you, you'd think you were out there being a superhero."

It could be taken as a compliment, but the undertone was as lovable as his smirk.

Aiden couldn't help but respond.

"Considering he saved my life, I think a superhero is an apt comparison."

Aiden heard his own condescending tone loud and clear. Both men turned to him. The detective dropped his smirk. He sat up straight and fixed him with a stare that didn't waver.

"Mr. Riggs. We meet two times in one day. Once at the morgue, and now you're here at the department." He shook his head. "Is it boredom?"

Aiden felt his eyebrow go sky-high.

"Excuse me?"

"All I'm saying is that boredom in a small town can be a powerful motivator to do some questionable things."

Aiden tilted his head to the side. He narrowed his gaze.

"Are you asking me if I planned to have a random guy attack me because I was bored? Or are you asking if I went to the morgue today looking for my friend because I was bored? Because surely as a detective you have better questions than that to ask."

Out of his periphery, Aiden saw Mack cover his mouth by running his hand along his jaw. He could have sworn it was to hide a smile, but his attention was sticking closer to Detective Winters. There was no trace of humor left in the man.

Good.

Aiden had offended him.

You offended me first, buddy.

"The timing is a bit weird, is all," Winters answered.

Aiden tamped down the urge to throw his hands wide and point out that the timing wasn't convenient to him, either, but Mack took the conversational reins before he could find an actual appropriate response.

"I already told Deputy McCoy what happened," he said to Winters. "And the only reason we were able to give you the suspect at all was because Mr. Riggs here was quick with his bat. I don't think boredom factored into anything at all."

Aiden sat up straighter. He nodded.

Detective Winters kept his unflattering expression.

He, at least, didn't try to be insulting again.

"That hit is now giving us a headache," he said. "Jonathan was bellyaching so much that he's at the hospital for a CT scan. Though I think he's just stalling for time so his cousin lawyer can get in from Knoxville."

Aiden already knew that Jonathan Smith had been the man beneath the hoodie. The first thing Mack had done after Aiden had wielded the bat was take his mask off. He'd identified him quickly and with a lot of disbelief. Aiden had never seen him before and didn't recognize the name.

"Deputy McCoy said Jonathan tried mugging someone last summer," Mack said. "Last I heard, he was working with his dad before that."

Detective Winters shook his head.

"His dad moved out of state to live with his sister. After that Jonathan fell in with the wrong crowd. Debt up to his eyeballs. He's been popping up on our radar ever since. Though what he did tonight has been the most extreme thing we've seen."

The two of them shared another knowing look.

Locals.

Aiden was most decidedly not on the same level as them.

"Then what happens now?" he asked. "We've already given statements."

Detective Winters sighed. He was over whatever glee he'd had when he had entered the room. Now he seemed tired.

"We'll call if we need you." He pointed to Aiden. "Until then, I don't want to run into you again, okay? Not here, the morgue or tying up any more of our resources. Got it?"

Aiden saw red again.

Why did he feel like he was being blamed for what happened?

His hands fisted and, despite the warning, he was about to see how much he could really offend the detective.

Mack, however, stood and spoke before Aiden could.

"We'll head out now. You have our numbers." Mack turned to Aiden. "Let's go."

For a second, Aiden wasn't sure he would, but then his brain betrayed him. He found himself standing and then followed Mack out of the room and right out to the parking lot. All without giving the detective another piece of his mind.

A regret he vented as soon as they were in the night air.

"I don't know what your relationship is with that guy, but he's the worst. He acts like me getting attacked is not only inconvenient to him but also something I enjoyed." Aiden felt his face twist in anger. "I'm already having a bad day. I don't need him to add to it."

Because there was nothing else he could physically do, Aiden shook his shoulders out with some vigor.

Mack didn't react at all.

Aiden glanced over. The taller man looked as displeased with their experience as he was.

Maybe even more so.

Aiden guessed he really didn't like the detective at all.

He took a long breath in and tried to redirect his anger back to appreciation.

"Well, once again, thanks for the save," he said. "Whether it was my bad luck or not, I appreciate it."

Mack nodded.

Then he walked away.

Aiden paused on the way to his car. After the deputies had shown up, Aiden had driven his hatchback to the department. Mack had ridden with him but had stayed silent other than giving directions. Now Aiden wondered how he would get back to his vehicle, wherever it was.

He opened his mouth to shout out to Mack's retreating back when Aiden realized he was walking toward a truck idling in a spot on the other side of the lot.

He shouldn't have been surprised.

Of course Mack Atwood had someone waiting on him.

Aiden watched as his savior walked around to the passenger's side of the truck. He sighed and turned to his empty hatchback.

He bet it would be a long time before he ever saw the oldest Atwood brother again.

THE SUN WAS out and shining the next morning when three things happened to disrupt Mack's attempt at peace. The first was his sister at his door just as dawn hit. Goldie was a sight to see as she fretted around his room, trying to get a more detailed story of what had happened the night before.

"That's awful," she'd exclaimed once Mack had been done with his retelling of the events. "I never thought Jonathan would do something like that."

She had gone off on a tangent about how they'd known Jonathan Smith since middle school before she'd revealed her original reason for coming in to see him so early.

"That poor Mr. Riggs," she'd said. "He hasn't even been in Willow Creek that long and he's already dealing with death and danger."

And Detective Winters, Mack had wanted to add.

"I heard that other than Mrs. Cole and her husband, he isn't social with anyone else," she'd continued, all mothering voice. "I think I'll invite him to eat with us today so he can see some Willow Creek kindness."

Mack had quickly been against the idea.

"I don't think that's necessary. He might just want to rest today."

But Goldie was already set on the idea.

"Not only has he been through an ordeal, from what you have said, it seems that he's a big reason why you didn't take another knife. That at the very least should get that man a meal as a thank-you. Plus, knowing you, you probably didn't even say the words *thank you* to him. Instead you just grumbled and maybe nodded once or twice."

Mack couldn't deny that. They both knew she was right.

And according to Aiden himself, he'd thumbed his nose at the help instead of being gracious.

Still, it didn't mean he was happy about the invite.

He was even less so when the second of three things happened.

Aiden actually accepted.

His little silver SUV came bouncing down the drive at eleven on the dot.

Mack stayed on the front porch and watched the procession. He didn't know what he expected of Aiden in the daylight, but all his attention wrapped around the man the second he was outside.

Particularly the bruises.

They stretched around Aiden's neck in an ugly contrast to his tanned skin. They weren't as angry as they could have been, but they were undeniably there.

Mack tried to ignore them.

He'd already done enough as it was. He had helped Aiden after all.

Yet, the closer Aiden got, the less Mack could pretend they weren't there.

He also couldn't ignore the rising anger in him.

Suddenly he was back in that parking lot the night before.

He should have been faster.

What he hadn't told Aiden or anyone else after was that he had been following the man already. By chance he had seen Aiden leaving his office across the street. It had felt like a fated event. Mack had questions and Aiden had his answers, but before he could leave to ask them, he had been delayed by a few goodbyes from partygoers.

By the time he made it across the street, Aiden had already turned the corner.

Mack had debated whether or not to follow him.

Then he'd thought better of it.

Was it his place to find out the identity of John Doe?

Did he need to learn more about Aiden Riggs?

No, on both parts.

He could alert the sheriff's department to the article with John Doe's picture and, as for Aiden, he could simply never see him again and be okay.

It wasn't like he was going to be in town for long anyways.

Then the car horn had gone off.

After he'd followed the sound and seen Aiden in danger, all of Mack's decisions came fast. He had been all instinct.

Once the danger had been over, he had tried his best to revert back to his self-isolation.

He'd even forgotten to ask about the picture or John Doe in the hustle that had followed. The thought hadn't even crossed his mind until he was sitting in Ray's truck outside the sheriff's department after leaving Detective Winters. He had watched Aiden's taillights disappear, then he had given the Bellwether Tech article to Ray and decided his involvement with Aiden Riggs was done.

That was that.

No more getting involved.

But, now, it felt like fate again.

Aiden Riggs was standing in front of him, smiling.

And all Mack could see were the bruises around his neck.

Staying out of Willow Creek's problems might be hard, but it was something Mack knew was doable.

Yet, at that moment, he realized something truly startling.

Avoiding Aiden Riggs's troubles?

That might not be something he could do.

Chapter Seven

Aiden had somehow found himself sitting opposite Mack Atwood again. This time, though, there were more Atwoods to go around.

"You can call me Goldie, by the way," Marigold said to him, settling into the seat to his right. "It's a nickname I wear more proudly than my real name. Plus, it sure sounds cute when these two here have to say it when they're being serious."

She pointed to Aiden's left at the last of the three Atwoods surrounding him. Finn was dressed casually, but he still seemed stylish. He smiled wide and chuckled. Aiden understood again why he was touted as charming.

"Don't let this nice talk fool you, Aiden," he said. "If anyone is scolding anyone in this family, it's Goldzilla here. I'm the mouth of the operation, Mack's the brawn and Goldie is the brains. She has a running list of those who offend her and all the ways she can dress them down later. May ye never get on that list."

Aiden heard the woman in question scoff, but his attention was on the oldest Atwood.

Mack was also dressed down to comfort. He wore a long-sleeved beige shirt and blue jeans that ran somewhere in the middle of the denim-colored spectrum. They looked good on him, as did his dark boots. The only thing that seemed a bit off was his eyes. Ever since Aiden had said hello on the front porch, Mack had been staring at him more but saying a whole lot less.

Aiden would have been self-conscious about it, but he was starting to think that all the extroverted genes in the family had been pulled out and stored in the Atwood twins. The mouth and the brains. The brawn had gotten the strength and silence of the wind.

"Oh, yeah, this one here is definitely the talker." Goldie passed Aiden a glass of sweet tea and pointed the spoon she had used to stir the sugar in at her twin. "He can sell water to a whale or drive you to sleep in total boredom if he wanted. It's why we only let him use his powers at work. He's too dangerous otherwise."

Finn waved the comment off.

"Everyone has a skill they lean on. I bet Aiden here has some serious technical know-how to be running his own business."

It wasn't a question but Aiden saw it as his intro into the conversation. They all started to eat lunch as he joined in.

"I won't lie, I do know my way around a computer," he said. "Some kids played outside—I was stuck to a computer screen. My grandma hated that…until I fixed her bridge club president's computer after she'd gotten a nasty virus. After that it was amazing how quickly she encouraged me."

Aiden laughed, and Finn and Goldie followed.

"I bet you scored her some serious cool points in the club," Finn said.

Aiden nodded.

"She became the president's go-to lady after that, and I, apparently, became their sect's IT guy. I even left a party once in college to walk a member through hooking up a printer on the phone." The smile was already there, but Aiden felt it widen at the memory. "My date at the time thought I was lying about who I was talking to. He didn't believe me until I had her on speakerphone. He didn't invite me out again after that."

Aiden expected a hesitation. It wasn't unusual to get one. So he averted his gaze to his food to give the moment some space in anticipation.

But there was none.

"His loss," Goldie said without missing a beat.

"And the bridge club's gain," Finn said. "I also feel like that would look really good on a résumé. 'Bridge club savior.' Probably a better extracurricular than most college kids can put down anyways."

A weight settled against Aiden's chest. Goldie and Finn seemed totally relaxed.

Aiden had met good people before, and he had met people he wished he hadn't. He had been ignored, overlooked and praised. He had been abandoned, and he had been loved.

Willow Creek wasn't different.

Someone had hurt him.

Yet someone had also saved him.

Aiden didn't look up at the man opposite him but he decided then that all three Atwoods were the kind of people who made things warm. He'd been nervous about accepting Goldie's invite, but now he was glad he had. The heaviness on his chest was the good kind of heavy.

Aiden felt his shoulders relax a little.

Mack, however, tested that relaxation quickly.

"Were you in the technology field before coming to Willow Creek?"

Mack was leveling him with a stare that was as steady as it was strong. Instead of a calming effect, those ocean-blue eyes made him anxious.

Mostly because he didn't like going anywhere near talk of Bellwether Tech.

So, he didn't.

"I was recruited to a big tech company in Nashville and worked there for a while," he skirted. "I'm sure a lot of people like the corporate feel, but I realized suits and corner offices didn't really hit the spot for me. That's why I came to Willow Creek to open Riggs Consulting. It seemed as far away from my last job as I could get."

Aiden hadn't meant to say the last part. He tried to amend it.

"You know, to get a better work-life balance."

Mack still didn't break eye contact.

"Why did you choose Willow Creek?" he asked. "It's not exactly a hot spot for entrepreneurs."

Aiden oddly felt like he was being accused of something. He tightened his smile.

"A coworker used to visit here a lot when he was younger. He talked it up so much that I decided to check it out myself after leaving the company. I guess you can tell that I was a fan." Aiden added a laugh. "It also helped that the rent for the office and my house here combined was still lower than my apartment in Nashville."

Finn nodded deep to that.

"Sue went looking at places to live there after competition and, well, she came back," he said.

"That might have been more of her mama's doing than

price," Goldie responded, looking thoughtful. She clapped her hands on the next breath, beaming. "Well, I'm sure glad you ended up picking our little town, Aiden. If not this guy here would have probably found himself in more trouble."

She motioned to Mack.

The man was still all eyes on Aiden.

It was really starting to grate.

He sidestepped Goldie's compliment and went straight at the man with no manners.

"You know, I realize now that I don't actually know what you do for your job. It must involve travel, since you said you're leaving again soon."

This time Mack had a reaction. It was subtle but there. Aiden couldn't tell if it was a flash of anger, annoyance or a grimace. Considering how Goldie swooped in, he guessed he had definitely said something he shouldn't have.

"He *just* got back. And I'm sure his boss won't let him take another contract until he's had time to decompress from the last job."

Mack switched his gaze finally.

"I'm the one who accepts the contracts. It's my boss's job to hand them to me when they come in. Not baby me."

Goldie wasn't amused.

For the first time since they had sat down to eat, she lost her smile completely.

Then it was a staring contest.

Maybe that was just how the Atwoods emoted. Intense staring surrounded by silence.

Finn was still cheery, at least.

"I'm a medical sales rep at the hospital. I stay local mostly, so it's not as exciting as Mack here. He's in the private security business and travels to wherever the clients are. He just got back from a job yesterday."

Mack swung his glare to his other sibling, but the damage was already done. Now Aiden understood Detective Winters's superhero comment.

"Oh, really?" Aiden said. "Private security. Is that kind of like the Secret Service for the president?"

Mack snorted.

Finn continued with the save.

"He's a bodyguard," he explained. "High-end. Top of the tier. You want him on your side for sure."

Aiden was impressed.

"Oh, how Hollywood-sounding of you."

Mack was *not* impressed.

He looked like a man ready to scold, mouth opening alongside a frown, but he stopped without a word coming out. Aiden heard the sound of crunching gravel a few beats after the rest of the table. His head was the last to turn toward the front of the house.

"You two expecting anyone?" Mack asked as he pushed his chair back.

Goldie and Finn shook their heads.

"I wouldn't be surprised if it was Ray," Finn said. "He's like a moth to a flame when you're in town."

It was a statement that sounded intimate, but Mack shook his head. He spoke as he went to the kitchen window over the sink.

"Ray had to go into work early today."

Aiden was wondering who exactly this Ray was when Mack cursed low. It was like he pushed a button that activated tension in the room. Even Aiden tightened in his seat.

"What?" Goldie and Finn asked in sync.

Mack gave another cuss.

"It's the sheriff."

"What?" The twins spoke in sync again, but Goldie was the first to hustle to the window.

"Why is he here?" She angled her chin up at Mack. "Does he want something else from you?"

Aiden felt his eyebrow rise. He had only met the sheriff once since setting up Riggs Consulting. He'd come with a few other business owners and made polite conversation while dropping a few mentions about his reelection campaign coming up. Past that Aiden hadn't had a reason or chance to talk to the man.

Apparently Mack had.

Even from where Aiden was sitting, he could see Mack's jaw clench.

A moment of quiet wove through the four of them.

Then Mack was quick.

He turned to Finn.

"See what he wants," he said. "Call me if it's something I need to come out for. If not, don't tell him we're here."

Finn stood at attention and nodded like it was a normal thing to say when the sheriff visited. And maybe it was for the Atwoods. For Aiden, though, he was more than confused by the procedure.

"Is there something wrong with the sheriff?"

Mack moved across the room to him in less than two steps, took both of their plates and then set them on the countertop out of sight from the rest of the room. The sound of a car door shutting from the direction of the front of the house got Finn to the window for a peek.

"He's always a candidate for election first, a sheriff second," Mack grumbled.

Goldie was smoothing down her hair.

"That's Mack-speak for he talks too much and smiles even more," she explained.

"He also has a habit of asking for favors," Mack added. "And since I've already done a big one for him since being back, I'm not going to set myself up for another."

The doorbell chime sounded through the house. All the Atwoods paused, like they were computer programs going through a temporary restart. Aiden used the momentary silence to question the trio.

"So, what am *I* supposed to do?"

Goldie and Finn might have been on the same page with their brother before, but at that question they looked to Mack for an answer, too.

Aiden had to give it to the bodyguard—for a big, muscled man, he was quick.

"You're coming with me."

THE SHERIFF CAME in through the front door as Mack led Aiden out the back. If the twins did their job right, they would keep him in the living room for the duration of his stay and he would never have the chance to walk past the few windows that showed them sneaking off. Then again, Sheriff Boyd had a knack for being sneaky when he wanted to.

That's why Mack's pace was quick as they headed across the yard, through the fence and out into the line of trees that separated the main house from most of the workable acreage. It wasn't until they were carving a path between oaks that he slowed. A beat after that, Aiden laughed.

"You must be a pretty good bodyguard," he said. "The way I just automatically followed you running *away* from the sheriff and then into some woods was effortless. You

must have a good 'I protect people for a living' aura coming off you."

Aiden brushed his arm as he made room for himself at
Mack's side.

Mack rolled his shoulder back and snorted.

"I'm not running away from anyone," he corrected.

"Ah, yes. Excuse me. You just happen to be giving me an
Atwood estate tour at a very convenient time." Aiden motioned to the trees around them. "Starting with this charming, secluded wooded area."

Mack didn't like being misunderstood. He cleared his
throat and picked up the pace again.

"This is the only path that all three of us take to get to
the barn," he said. "You'll be thankful for the shade when
it gets really hot out in the peak of summer."

"Oh, so you're saying there's going to be a next time for
us in these here woods?"

It was an off-the-cuff comment, a little joke that seemed
to be part of Aiden Riggs's style, but Mack almost lost
his footing at how comfortably it came out. In fact, he'd
already been taken aback by Aiden's level of ease at the
kitchen table. Mack would never be one to boast about the
Atwood status around town, but he knew there was a certain nervousness that usually followed anyone who came to
the house for a social visit. If not for the twins' popularity
around town, that anxiousness came because of Mack and
what had happened after the warehouse fire.

Yet, Aiden had settled among them all and answered
every question, kept up with the conversation and even
shared personal details they hadn't asked for. He also hadn't
backed down at Mack's stare.

The man wasn't afraid.

That could be an indication of innocence.

That could also be an indication of guilt.

Confidence went both ways, after all.

Mack shook his head a little and tried to ignore Aiden's playfulness.

He stopped in his tracks.

Aiden took a few steps longer before he followed suit. He turned around and gave Mack a questioning look.

Even without his stylish party clothes, he stood out to Mack. Like someone had a spotlight tracking him.

It was unnerving.

It was also annoying.

Mack needed answers to get rid of both encroaching feelings.

He decided to dive right in.

"Did you used to work with Bryce Anderson?"

Aiden's eyebrow rose higher, but he didn't hesitate.

"Yeah, briefly," he said with a nod. "Why?"

"Were you close?"

This time his brows drew together, his nose scrunching between his eyes.

"I wouldn't say so. I saw him a few times in the office and even less times than that outside it. We haven't even talked since I quit the company." Aiden's hair shifted as he tilted his head to the side a little. "Why? How do you know Bryce Anderson?"

Mack could have lied. He could have avoided the question altogether. He could have kept asking his own as a distraction. Yet, he saw something in Aiden's answer that made him decide to not back away from the truth.

Sincerity.

In that moment Mack believed Aiden had had nothing to do with whatever had happened at the park.

So he told the truth.

"The John Doe you tried to identify yesterday was Bryce Anderson," he said, ripping the Band-Aid off. "I was able to identify him through a Bellwether Technologies company photo at the party last night. That's why I got to you so fast when you were attacked. I was coming to talk to you about it."

Aiden's expression turned to shock and stayed that way after Mack finished.

Then something peculiar happened.

Aiden didn't say a word.

For a moment, Mack respected the silence. It was a lot to process, even if they hadn't been close, but then that silence kept going.

And then Mack realized it wasn't silence at all.

It was Aiden Riggs making a plan.

One that apparently included him now.

Aiden reached out and grabbed Mack's elbow.

"I know you're a bodyguard, but can I hire you to help me find someone instead?"

Chapter Eight

There was an old Ford truck at the barn, rusted along the bumper and what must have been slick red paint when it was new now chipped here and there across the body. The tires were maintained, as was the interior. Though Aiden smelled a faint scent of smoke from the passenger seat cushion as he settled in.

Mack didn't explain the vehicle and started the engine with confidence. A confidence that didn't extend to him.

"I don't take personal contracts," he said for the second time. It had been only five minutes since Aiden had made the request, but it really seemed to have grated. Mack had huffed and puffed before turning him down the first time. "Even though I work for someone, I'm still considered a freelancer," he continued. "I only take what they assign me and then of those only what I'm comfortable with. Finding someone isn't on the list of skills I offer."

Aiden tamped down the urge to smile. The bodyguard was being so serious with his words yet failing in his actions.

"Then where are we going?"

Together they glanced at the sticky note in Mack's right hand. It was the address the anonymous email sent to Riggs

Consulting had come from. The location Aiden had planned to visit after lunch.

Until Mack had found another connection to Bellwether Tech.

Bryce Anderson.

Dead.

Murdered.

The moment Aiden had heard that, his brain had crunched the numbers on several scenarios. It just so happened that the man who had been towering over him in the woods had been his best chance at finding the truth. Or, at least, finding a direction to turn.

What Aiden *hadn't* planned on when asking for help was Mack actually agreeing to take him to the address while skirting the sheriff.

All while grumbling that he wouldn't help.

Mack took the note and tossed it over to Aiden now. There was still some grumbling in his words.

"I'm not helping look for anyone," he said. "I just happen to know where that place is and how much of a pain in the backside it is for nonlocals to get there. This isn't helping. It's courtesy."

Once again Aiden had to keep his smile under wraps.

"Ah," he said. "So it's all about good manners, then."

Mack pulled his phone from his pocket and nodded.

"Us Atwoods have a reputation to uphold in this town, after all."

He sent a quick text to someone before they started driving down a gravel path from the barn. It curved away from the direction of the house, too, until there was nothing but trees on either side for scenery.

"Will the sheriff come after you if he sees you leaving?"

Aiden pictured the sheriff pursuing them in a high-speed chase while Mack just kept yelling out the window about not wanting to help anyone.

"We're taking the scenic route to the entrance. I texted Finn and told him we were leaving this way. He'll cover for us." There was that confidence again. Mack was a man unbothered while being a man who had become extremely bothered by Aiden's request.

He was a walking contrast.

One that surely had Aiden's attention.

"I can't believe I've been in Willow Creek for six months and not run into him and Goldie before. They seem like great allies to have in your corner."

Mack snorted.

Aiden thought he'd retort with something sarcastic. Instead there was a notable change in his tone. It was deeper. More serious.

"It is surprising you haven't seen them before. You must work a lot to almost completely miss the Willow Creek social scene."

He wasn't asking a question but there was definite space for an answer.

Aiden had expected as much. He'd also be asking his fair share had their situations been reversed.

"Yeah, I tend to get lost a lot," Aiden admitted. "In my work, I mean. Especially after hours. There's just something about the light of a computer screen in the dead of night. Sometimes Mrs. Cole has come in for work in the morning and I've still been up clicking away. It's not the best schedule for being social."

"I guess you couldn't do the same thing at your last job."

There it was. Mack's link to the topic of Bellwether Tech.

Aiden shifted in his seat slightly. The trees around them started to thin as the gravel road curved slightly.

"It was an eight-to-five job with some overtime depending on the project. It's definitely different from my hours now."

What he wasn't saying filled Aiden's mind. He didn't dare let it spill out of his mouth. While he had asked Mack for help, he wasn't going to tell him everything that had gone wrong in his life.

Mack didn't need to know the real reason Aiden had left the company.

Mack turned his head, but Aiden wasn't sure if he was looking to the drive that branched off and went to the main house or checking his expression. Either way, Aiden put all his effort into a nonchalant smile.

One that said everything was fine and normal and not worthy of deeper conversation.

Although there was still Leighton to consider. Mack was quick to bounce over to him.

"And this guy that you think sent the email still works there? At Bellwether?"

"As far as I know. I haven't talked to him in a while, but he would have told me if he had quit."

Of that Aiden was sure. If only because of how Leighton and he had ended things.

"So you two are close."

It was another statement that required an answer.

Aiden nodded.

"We used to be."

If the sheriff saw them leaving through the main gate, he didn't come racing down the drive to follow them. Mack took the turn onto the main street and got them going toward town. Aiden almost thought the conversation was over until Mack continued.

"What happened between you two? You and this guy?"

That caught Aiden off guard.

"That's mighty personal there."

Mack wasn't budging.

"If he really is in danger and was the one who sent the email, then he's asking you for help or at the very least confiding in you," he started. "And you, someone who just said he isn't as close as he used to be with him, are investigating despite a potentially-connected current homicide and an unrelated violent attack. Both of which took place only yesterday. I just can't help but be curious as to what happened between you two that made your closeness cool. And how, even despite that fact, you two are trusting a whole lot in one another."

It was the most Aiden had heard Mack Atwood say in one go.

It also made his question reasonable.

That didn't mean it had an easy answer.

Aiden opened his mouth to respond, but what was he going to say? His mind went blank, then into overdrive looking for a vague answer that would stop any more questions.

Luckily, he didn't have to make a choice.

Mack slowed significantly. At first Aiden assumed it was because of the road. The route to the Atwood estate was no joke. It had taken almost twenty minutes to go three miles and, of those twenty minutes, Aiden had white-knuckled the steering wheel the entire time. The road had wound its way up the mountainous terrain where at any given moment there was a drop covered by trees on one side of the vehicle and a wall of rock on the other. Aiden had already thought with conviction that there was no way he would have ever driven the path at night or while it rained.

However, now Mack was slowing down and saying something beneath his breath.

Aiden focused past his internal self-conflict and realized the reason for the decrease in speed wasn't caution. It was because they were being forced to stop.

A shiny black truck was parked in the left lane with flashers on. Orange cones were set up behind it and in the right lane. There was a man leaning against the hood wearing a hazard vest over jeans and boots. When he saw them, he pushed off and made a stop motion with his hand.

"Roadwork?" Aiden guessed.

They were at a portion of the road that was more straight than curvy. The truck was parked next to a guardrail that separated it from a drop and the woods that stretched between them and the main part of town.

Mack came to a stop but not too close to the man.

"It sure is a fancy truck for work," he said, putting them into Park.

The man in the vest gave a thumbs-up before motioning to Mack to come to him.

"Stay in the car," Mack ordered. "I'll handle this."

Aiden was surprised he listened so quickly, but, then again, Mack probably knew whoever it was. He watched as the two greeted each other, friendly enough. The worker pointed to the trees and then the road. Aiden couldn't see Mack's face but saw his shoulders shake in laughter— something Aiden realized he would have liked to see up close—before the two directed their attention back at him.

His face heated at the sudden interest. Then he noticed a car had driven up behind them and stopped, also waiting.

The worker nodded to Mack, said something else that got a smile from the man and then he was walking back to the truck.

However, he didn't go to the driver's side. Instead he walked around the hood and opened the passenger's door.

He was still smiling.

It didn't match the complete ice in his tone.

"I want you to stay calm but listen to everything I'm about to say. Okay?"

Mack made a show of pointing past him to the trees and then the road, just as the worker had.

"Put your hand on the gearshift but keep looking where I'm pointing."

As if Mack's orders were king, Aiden's body went on autopilot. He slid his hand over and grasped the gearshift knob. In tandem Mack draped himself between the body of the truck and the open door.

In any other circumstance, Aiden would have believed him to be relaxed.

"Unbuckle your seat belt. Don't worry about being obvious with it. They want us out of the truck."

With his right hand, Aiden complied again. This time, though, he had to question it.

"The worker said he wants us to leave the truck? Why?"

Mack surprised him with an exaggerated laugh.

His voice dropped so low that Aiden's adrenaline spiked before Mack gave him the bottom line.

"This is a trap, and I'm pretty sure him and the car behind us are about to try and take you, so I'm going to take you first." The statement was so fast and so blunt that Aiden couldn't form the words to question it. Not that Mack gave him the room. He had another order waiting, and it made the spike of adrenaline in Aiden turn into a surge.

"On the count of three, you're going to put the truck in Neutral—that's two clicks backward on the shifter—and then I need you to jump out and run into the trees behind us. No stopping, just running. Got it?"

Movement caught Aiden's eye. This time in the rearview mirror. The driver of the car behind them had opened their door.

All of Mack tensed.

Aiden knew their time had already run out. So did Mack.

"Three."

One word and absolute chaos.

Aiden downshifted the gear two clicks while Mack threw open the door as wide as it would go. The second the truck went into Neutral it started to roll. Fear that he wouldn't be able to exit the vehicle without falling or getting tangled up wrapped around Aiden. Just as Mack's hand wrapped around his arm.

The force was startling, but Mack pulled him out in one fluid move.

Then the yelling started.

Followed closely by the running.

Aiden went to the edge of the road, fully ready to go into the trees, but he stopped short.

The trees were there, but so was a drop.

It wasn't total, but the slope was significant enough that Aiden forgot Mack's instruction completely.

There was no way he could run down it; even if he could have seen where the slope led, the journey to get there wouldn't be a fun ride.

There had to be another way.

There had to be another path.

There—

A hand, warm and strong, wrapped around Aiden's.

Then Mack was off the edge of the road in a flash.

Hand in hand, they ran as fast as they could and made their escape.

Chapter Nine

If they had been a hundred yards farther up the road, Lover's Ledge would have saved them. It had a cliff overhang but that only stood over a drop that totaled four feet before hitting a stretch of even terrain. *That* would have been okay to run, jump and fall off, no problem.

But, no.

Mack had fallen into a trap that butted up against one hell of a hill covered in trees.

Keeping his footing was hard enough.

Keeping his footing while attached to another man was impossible.

They made it past the first oak, and then Aiden was a goner. His hand ripped out of Mack's as he fell. The imbalance made an already bad situation worse. Mack went down hard.

If they were at Lover's Ledge? The fall would have been quick and final.

They would have stuck in place.

But this wasn't Lover's Ledge.

Mack's fall became a roll, a violent tangle of limbs and speed. He tried to grab onto something—anything—to stop, but the world continued to be a painful blur.

Then the ground disappeared altogether.

Mack didn't have time to think, react or brace as he dropped over what must have been another ledge.

The ground met him again soon after.

A few seconds later, he met something else.

Mack hit the side of a raised clump of dirt and tree roots that stopped his momentum instantly. Air left his lungs. Pain filled him.

There wasn't time to think about either.

He could see the incline he had just come down. Aiden was still falling and coming down fast.

Mack didn't have a thought in his head after seeing that.

He moved faster than he ever had before and got into the path of Aiden's descent.

He readied to catch the man. There was no time to brace himself.

All Mack could do was take as much of the impact between the tree and Aiden.

And that's what he did.

Aiden slammed into Mack.

Mack didn't register the pain. He fastened his arms around the man as best he could.

The tree behind him came next.

Then that was it.

No sooner did he have Aiden in his arms, the world Mack knew went absolutely dark.

THE WORLD WAS FLOATING. It was trees and leaves and dirt and pain all just floating around him. It was also warm. Aiden sucked in breath after breath. His ribs ached. His ankle throbbed. Something was wrong with his face. It was cut or bruised or some combination of the two. It hurt. It all hurt.

There was also that warmth. It ran along his back, but it was the only thing that wasn't pulsing with pain. With great effort he caught his breath and craned his head around the best he could to see what he was sitting up against.

Then the world finally settled.

Dark hair, slack face.

"Mack!"

Aiden couldn't maneuver correctly after that. He tried to scramble off the man while also turning to face him, but his body was all awkward movements. Disjointed. He tipped over and his shoulder connected with the leaves beneath them. He yelled out as the pain in his ribs radiated from it. But Aiden wasn't slowing. He had a new urgency in him. It ratcheted higher every second that Mack wasn't saying something.

Finally, Aiden managed to roll over and sit himself up.

His stomach fell the second he was able to get a good look at Mack.

Where Aiden suspected that his face had met an angry fate on their fall, there was absolutely no denying that Mack's had taken a definite beating. His lip was busted, his right eyebrow, too, and a nasty bruise would take over one eye in the near future. His body hadn't fared much better. At least, not his clothes. His shirt was ripped long across the middle, his jeans torn in patches at the thigh. On first glance, there were no obvious broken bones or injuries that needed immediate attention, but that was to say nothing about the blood above Mack's hairline.

That and the fact that the man wasn't moving at all.

"Mack?" This time Aiden lowered his voice.

Mack didn't move an inch.

Aiden took a deep breath and held his index finger beneath Mack's nose. He was frozen as he waited.

"Come on," Aiden whispered again. "Be okay."

Like the command willed it, air pressed against his finger.

Mack was breathing.

Mack was alive.

Aiden could have cried.

"Thank you," he told the big man.

He rolled back and sank to the ground. The adrenaline he'd been carrying was crashing. He needed to pause for a second and get his bearings. He needed to—

A man shouted somewhere far off. Aiden couldn't make out exactly what was said but it was enough to remind him why it was they were in this predicament in the first place. He turned toward the path that they had fallen down. Aiden didn't know the landscape enough to make the best guess at how far down they were from the road. Maybe one hundred yards? Two hundred? More? All he could see was the small ledge above them in the distance.

Even if the men from the road wanted to follow them, they'd have to take their time to avoid the leaf-covered ski slope and mini cliff.

That would give Aiden some time to try and get help.

He got to his feet with greater effort than before and went for his cell phone in his front pocket.

It wasn't there.

Aiden patted the rest of his pockets. It was nowhere.

"No." He whirled around in their immediate area, eyes scanning the ground.

Nothing.

Aiden followed the path he had taken down after the ledge.

No luck. The phone must have come out somewhere in the fall.

He cussed to the trees.

Getting into Mack's jean pockets next wasn't easy, and it certainly wasn't fruitful. If he'd had his phone on him, it was long gone.

Another shout sounded again. Aiden couldn't tell if it was closer or not.

Would they really come this far down to get them?

And who were the men to begin with? Were they really after Aiden? If so, why?

Aiden's eyes traced Mack's face. He lingered there for a moment.

He shouldn't be surprised by now, but there it was, the feeling of something new and unexpected.

Aiden didn't know what was going on, but he knew the second Mack had come back to the truck that he had been working on pure instinct. An instinct that had told him that Aiden was in trouble. An instinct that had sent them over the side of a mountain without hesitation.

An instinct that Aiden trusted.

He didn't know why the men were after him, but Aiden was sure of one thing.

Mack had put his life on the line to protect him.

Now it was Aiden's turn.

Chapter Ten

There was a thumping.

Mack blinked against his confusion, then his pain. He went to touch the part of him that hurt the most but hit something on the way to his head.

"Hey!"

It was the perfect example of a loud whisper, and it came from behind him.

Against him.

"Don't say anything," the voice continued. Mack felt the vibration through his back. He blinked several more times, trying to figure out why until the thing he'd hit moved.

It was an arm, and it was wrapped around his chest.

It was Aiden's arm around him.

"Are you *holding* me?" Mack's voice came out broken. It hurt his head to talk. He knew without touching it that there was definitely blood somewhere above his forehead.

He tried to move, but Aiden tightened his hold.

He shifted until he was speaking at Mack's ear.

"I've just burned a billion calories dragging you *away* from danger," he whispered. "And I have no idea where I am and I can't tell if those guys are close to us anymore, so instead of getting your pride in a tizzy, can you help me listen?"

The scenery made more sense now.

Mack looked up and saw trees, not the ledge they had rolled off. The sunlight was also coming from a different direction. They had indeed moved. He could see the trail in the leaves and dirt that Aiden must have made while moving him.

The thumping also made sense now, too.

It was Aiden's heartbeat coming through Mack's back. It was racing.

Mack cleared his throat and nodded. He closed his eyes again and listened. For a moment all he heard was Aiden's breathing, then a few birds. Leaves shifting in a breeze that went over the treetops.

Aiden breathing again.

Mack opened his eyes.

"I don't hear anything."

Mack felt Aiden's relief in an exhale. The hold around his chest loosened.

"I heard them yelling earlier and didn't like how out in the open we were," Aiden said. He wasn't whispering, but he was notably more quiet. "I got us maybe five minutes away from where we were before I gave out. I don't know if you know this, but you're a big guy. If anyone tries to kidnap you, just play dead and I bet they'd leave you alone."

Standing up was a chore all its own, but untangling from Aiden while doing it was a pain. Not being sarcastic back to him was also a struggle. Mack tamped the urge down as he righted. Last time he had seen Aiden, he'd been trying to absorb his impact from a tree; now it was Aiden who had been between him and one. He held his hand out to Mack for assistance.

Before he agreed to it, Mack looked the man up and down.

Aiden had been lucky, at least on the outside. His clothes were torn in a few places and there were some scratches along his exposed skin, but none seemed too deep. There was dirt on his face and a bruise was no doubt forming along his jaw but, all in all, the man looked in good shape.

But the wince that contorted his face when Mack pulled him to stand definitely wasn't great.

"What hurts?" Mack asked, taking a step back to survey him again.

Aiden cradled his left side but gave a wry smile.

"Everything, but my ribs are really giving the rest of me a run for my money," he said. "I'm not a medical expert, but I'm guessing they're either bruised or broken. And, since I'm breathing okay and not unconscious, if they broke, then they didn't puncture anything." Aiden's gaze went somewhere above Mack's forehead. "What about you? You definitely were knocked out."

Mack snorted and motioned to his head.

"I've had worse."

Mack waited for a long-winded retort, but Aiden simply nodded.

"Good. Because I need you to tell me in a completely confident way that you know where we are and how to get us out of here without running into more trouble. Or, worse, another mountainous slip and slide."

It was a reasonable request, yet the way Aiden said it shifted something in Mack. Aiden needed his help, and it made sense that he would. Mack was a local, and he did know the area they were in.

Yet, that wasn't all.

Mack didn't just want to keep Aiden safe, he truly wanted to comfort him. He wanted him to believe in him.

"I do know how to get us out of here," he said, making sure his voice was even and strong. He motioned to his right. "The road is back up that way."

Aiden nodded.

"I didn't want to jostle you too much, so I dragged you as much in a straight line as I could from where we fell."

Mack turned to the opposite direction. He used to know the woods better than most locals, especially as a teen, but it had been a while since he had explored them with Ray or the twins. He imagined an aerial view of the mountainside. He knew where Lover's Ledge was. At least roughly. Which meant he knew with about the same certainty what was behind them. From there he could guess what direction led them to something useful. If he was right about where they currently were, then if they kept straight and went down the mountain they would either hit the no-outlet Cayman's Loop or...

A part of Mack hoped he had no idea where they were.

Out of every inch of Willow Creek, it would be simply cruel to be forced to see that place again.

Mack shook the possibility off.

The more he thought about it, he imagined them slightly more to the east.

"We need to walk down the mountain before we can get to anything. We're on the opposite side of where the road leads, but if we keep going this way, we should come to Cayman's Loop. It leads to a street that branches off from the main one that leads into downtown."

Aiden's eyebrow rose.

"Cayman's Loop? That sounds like a nightclub."

"It's an outlet with some houses along it. They took some storm damage years ago and never got repaired, so they're

empty, but the road will be good enough for us to follow."
A thought occurred to him. "Do you have your cell phone?"

Aiden sighed.

"I did before I turned into a rolling stone," he said. "I'm
assuming you lost yours in the fall, too."

Mack didn't have to check.

"I put mine in the truck's cupholder before we ever
stopped." He cussed low. "Unless those guys left it and
the truck on the road, it'll be a bit before the twins realize we're missing. Let's get going so we're not out here at
night. We have a decent walk if we don't want to fall again."
Mack's head throbbed as if to agree with him that he didn't
need any more fall damage, but he pushed through the discomfort to start their trek. Aiden fell into step without a
word. His gait sounded off, though he moved well enough
along the leaves.

That silence didn't last long, though. No more than ten
feet from their starting point, Aiden became chatty.

"I have a lot of questions but I want to ask about the
truck thing first."

Mack already knew what was coming.

"You mean why did I get you to put it in Neutral?"

Aiden snapped his fingers.

"Bingo."

It was Mack's turn to let out an exhale that dragged.

"They took the time to set a trap, to get a vest and cones
and set it all up on the road. The guy even made up some
weak excuse about needing to take down some branches.
He even small-talked me about the weather. So I figured
they were trying to be more stealth than open aggression."

"So you sent a truck their way hoping they'd deal with
it first before coming for us."

It was a good guess and the truth.

Mack nodded.

"You gambled," Aiden added. He laughed. "I guess it's always the quiet ones who do the unexpected."

Mack glanced over at the man. He was still holding his side but held on to his smile for a moment. Most people in their situation would be a mess. Aiden Riggs was somehow finding humor.

"I thought our chances were better than if I'd tried to drive away," he admitted. "I think there were more people in the truck, plus there was the guy in the car."

They had been outnumbered, and Mack hadn't known by how much. That was enough to get him worried. The gun he'd caught a glimpse of on the man wearing the vest? If he had one, who was to say the others didn't? Could they have driven away without finding out?

Mack hadn't been sure. So he had gone to a different extreme.

He had forced them to juggle while basically jumping off a cliff.

When Goldie found out about this, she would surely kill them.

Mack's mood plummeted. He hoped the men didn't think about going to the house. There would be hell to pay if so. He sidestepped over a large outcropping of tree roots. He slowed until he heard Aiden clear them, too, then returned to his faster clip.

"I guess it would be silly to think they were after you for some kind of vengeance," Aiden said. "Like someone you ticked off on a bodyguard job or a romantic betrayal that led some powerful group of unknowns to come after you? You know, all movie-like."

Mack had to snort at that.

"Negative. I'm going to say this is about you and not me."

Aiden was quiet a moment. When he spoke again, he seemed to have sobered.

"Bryce was killed, Leighton is missing and I was sent an email pinning blame on Bellwether Tech," he summarized. "You're right. All signs point back to me."

The ground started to slope more. Mack slowed again. He was hyperaware of where Aiden was in proximity to him. He wasn't about to let the man fall again. It was already a miracle both of them could even walk at the moment.

"And you were attacked last night, too," Mack pointed out.

"Do you think that's related? Don't you know that guy, though? Wait, did you recognize the worker guy just now, too?"

Mack usually disliked when people kept asking him if he recognized someone. Right now he was angry at himself that he hadn't.

"I've never seen the men at the road before, but we can't rule out Jonathan's involvement. It's too coincidental." And Mack had every intention of asking Jonathan his own set of questions the second he could. Until then he had to make do with the man of the hour. Though he felt himself hesitate a little. Being too blunt didn't feel right at the moment, so Mack tried repeating Aiden's earlier humorous attempt.

"Did something happen at Bellwether Tech to make someone vengeful against you? Did *you* tick someone off or pull off a romantic betrayal that got a target put on your back?"

There Mack was again, waiting for some sarcastic back-and-forth. Yet, all he got was silence.

It stretched.

When Aiden finally responded, it wasn't sarcastic at all. It was cold.

"I was the one betrayed."

Mack stopped in his tracks.

"What?"

Aiden didn't meet his eye as he faced him. His arm was still around his side, but the other hand was balled into a fist held low. His jaw was clenched.

It was such a contrast to the man before. Mack didn't know how to feel about it, either. Was he talking about his ex? His former job? Someone else? How big was the picture around Aiden Riggs that Mack still needed to step back farther to be able to see?

"What do you mean?" he repeated.

Green eyes found their way to his, a slow slide up.

Mack couldn't help himself. He took a step closer, the urge to reach out nearly overwhelming. Touching the man wouldn't give him answers, but he wanted to regardless.

Aiden's jaw unclenched. The tension that had built a cage around him stayed.

"I know I owe you of all people an explanation, but I can't give that," he said. "Not until we know for sure that I'm really in the middle of this."

Mack glanced down to see his other hand ball into a fist.

"Waiting to tell me what's going on could put you in more danger." Mack leveled his gaze with the man again. Those green eyes were trees that made up a forest.

Trees that stayed absolutely rooted with conviction.

Aiden's voice was clear and even when he spoke again.

"Waiting to tell you might put me in danger, but telling you? That's a guarantee that you'll be stuck right in there with me." Aiden motioned behind Mack. "Help me get to town and then I can do the rest."

He took a step around Mack and started back down the mountain.

Mack watched him for a moment.

Aiden had just let him off the hook, cleared him of the obligation to help. Mack should have felt relieved. He should have been more than glad that for once someone hadn't pushed him to help with their problems. That he had been given the okay to leave when his next task was done.

So why did he feel more hooked than ever?

Chapter Eleven

Aiden was staring out from the tree line and trying not to let the growing darkness above make him anxious. They'd finally made it to the bottom of the mountain. That was a win, no matter how tiring, painful or awkward it had been.

And it had been all three.

Mostly because the two of them hadn't said more than a few words during their trek downward. Aiden refusing to tell Mack anything about his past had done in their conversational relationship. The only talking they had managed in the last few hours was related to what they were doing in the moment.

Watch out for this hole.

Make sure to hold on to this tree while going around it.

Lean back while walking down this slope to keep from falling.

I hope we can beat the rain.

The sky overhead was still a threat, but the rain had held off so far. Aiden hoped their luck on that front kept going. Their luck on the other pressing matter? He wasn't so sure.

"Do you think we'll run into them?" Aiden asked Mack. The bodyguard had been scanning the field past their hiding place for a minute or two without a word. "The men from the road."

Aiden could take the silence during their journey to flat land—mainly because it was his fault—but now he wanted to hear Mack. He needed to hear him to keep his nerves in check.

Mack obliged, but only after heaving a big sigh.

"I grew up in Willow Creek and have lived on this mountain for almost my entire life, and I still don't know exactly where I am. If they manage to find us now, then hats off to them." He pointed ahead. "I'm thinking that Cayman's Loop is past that outcropping of trees, though. We won't have cover as we go to it, so let's be fast just in case."

"And what's the plan again when we get to Cayman's Loop?"

Mack turned his face up toward the sky.

"We follow the road to downtown, keeping to the shoulder, which should have some more trees for cover. Even if it doesn't, we should be able to hear someone driving up for most of the road."

"And if it's not Cayman's Loop?"

Aiden thought it was a valid question.

Mack ignored it.

"Are you ready?" he asked instead. "We need to go."

There was no time to answer. Mack was out in the open and moving quickly. Aiden followed. He wasn't the only one. The time it took them to make it to the next group of trees timed perfectly with a crackling sound that sent chills down Aiden's spine.

Thunder.

It even made Mack pause.

"We might need to use one of the houses as a shelter so we don't get caught in the rain," he said over his shoulder as they moved through the trees. "Trying to make it on foot to town while it's pouring is borrowing trouble we don't need."

Aiden had started watching the ground between him and Mack, trying to be careful not to trip. While he believed his injuries were all minor, he didn't want to collect more.

However, he ran smack-dab into a wall of muscle and silence before he realized that Mack hadn't just stopped talking, he had stopped moving, too.

"What?" Aiden asked after bouncing back and pawing at his forehead. When Mack didn't react to the hit, Aiden dropped his voice into a panicked whisper. "What is it? What's happening?"

Aiden peeked around Mack's shoulder.

The trees had thinned. In the distance was a building. It wasn't a house, and it stood alone. Half of the structure had crumbled, but the other half seemed sturdy enough to protect them if the rain set in. Relief started to pool in Aiden's chest. He was also just glad to see something other than trees.

A sentiment Mack didn't share.

"Cruel."

It was one word, and Aiden wasn't even sure he'd heard the other man right.

"Cruel?"

Mack didn't move.

"Cruel," he repeated.

Aiden stepped closer and tried to figure out what Mack meant. What was cruel? That they weren't at Cayman's Loop? There were no other buildings that Aiden could see? Maybe that was what Mack was taking so hard.

Yet, the second Aiden took in the bodyguard's expression, he had no idea what was going on.

Mack was a quiet man. That had been obvious since the moment they met. Sure, he chatted when he needed to, but he very much seemed a man who thought more than he ever spoke. A quality that, if Aiden was being honest, he wished he himself could master. That quiet, however, had a rhythm to it. Others ebbed, Mack Atwood flowed.

Now, that quiet man seemed absolutely hollow.

Not quiet by choice. Quiet by circumstance.

By anger? Pain? Something else that Aiden couldn't understand since he had only known the man two days?

Standing there, staring up at Mack's new quiet, Aiden believed he was right.

Whatever had happened, whatever had caused it, something in Mack had broken the moment he had seen the building.

And when the rain started, Mack's broken stayed just as broken.

Aiden put his hands over his head.

"We need to get some cover," he said. "Let's go."

The rain went from light to pouring within the space of his words, and still Mack's refused to move.

"I'll walk to town," he said. His voice was stone. "You can go stay in there."

His hands were useless as cover. Aiden shook his head.

"If you're going to town, I'm going with you."

"It's too dangerous. Just stay there."

Mack started to walk. Aiden panicked and grabbed his elbow. He raised his voice to make sure he could be heard over the rain.

"We either go in there," he said, pointing to the building, "or we walk to town *together*. Those are the only two options."

Lightning flashed, and thunder boomed right after. It was so loud that it reverberated in his chest. Aiden tightened his grip on Mack's arm.

He couldn't be sure, but he thought Mack said "Cruel" again.

What he did know was the man made a decision.

And he wasn't a fan of it.

"Fine."

They walked toward the structure, and Aiden could see it was a warehouse. Or used to be. It was also a lost cause. Water and fire damage, missing walls and half of the roof crumbled, broken and boarded windows. Even the side door wasn't closed all the way.

Aiden was about to see if the inside was as severe, but Mack grabbed his hand before he could open the door fully.

"We can wait out here," he said, motioning to the overhang above them. Like the building, it had seen better days, but the part over the door, and what must have once been a loading dock, was still intact. Still, Aiden wasn't sure it was smart to stay outside. He said as much.

"It would be a shame to survive our exciting romp down the mountain only to be done in by lightning." Aiden tried to go for the door again. Mack didn't let go of his grip. Instead he pulled against it.

"This place has been abandoned for almost twenty years. It's not safe." Mack pulled Aiden away from the door, then he dropped down to sit on the concrete near it. "Let's stay out here."

Aiden's hand was still wrapped in Mack's grip. Aiden looked down his arm at the man. He seemed smaller. It pulled at Aiden. He sighed but nodded.

"I basically followed you off a cliff earlier, so why would

I go against your instincts now?" Aiden lowered himself to the ground. Mack let go of his hand after he settled. He was staring ahead of them, out at the rain. From where he sat, Aiden could see a sliver of a parking lot to his right. There was a whole bunch of nothing in front of them and to the left. Aiden wasn't used to running into so much open space and trees. Where he had lived in Nashville had been blocks of tight living spaces and offices.

It was nice to have an open place to breathe.

It would have been nicer had people not been chasing them to get here.

"Do you think anyone knows something's up with us?" Aiden asked. "I mean, that we're missing and not that just out and about. Though, are we considered missing if we know where we are?"

Mack only moved his lips when he answered. The rest of him seemed to have hardened along with his mood.

"It depends on the truck and the sheriff. If the truck was found empty and the twins found out about it, they would have started the search. If the sheriff kept talking with them for a while or asked for a favor that got them away from the house, then they might not have had the time to reach out or realize I'm not with my phone."

It was clear he'd been thinking about this for some time. Aiden's mind while coming down the mountain had been filled, too, but mostly with Bellwether Tech and Leighton. He hadn't been as practical as the bodyguard, apparently.

"Then there's the possibility that those guys made the truck disappear, so even if the twins realize we're missing, they probably have no idea where to look," he added. "I wouldn't think to look off the side of the mountain first. I definitely wouldn't think to look here."

He put emphasis on the word *here*. So much so that Aiden focused on it rather than their predicament.

"You said this place has been abandoned for almost twenty years. I'm surprised it hasn't been demolished and the land used for something else. When I first was looking at places to live in Willow Creek, the Realtor showed me some plots of land that were wildly expensive. I bet this one would go for a ton of money."

Mack didn't skip a beat.

"The owner won't sell."

It was a steel gate slamming down on the conversation. Aiden tried to respect it. He had, after all, been the one to shut Mack down about his past in the woods. Demanding small talk now would make him a hypocrite.

So Aiden tried to focus on other things.

The rain was heavy and steady. It wasn't getting better, but it wasn't getting worse. He was starting to get cold from his wet clothes, but his side and chest bothered him the most. Aiden went back to cradling his ribs again, though it didn't do much to help the pain. He sucked in a breath as he readjusted and was glad that Mack couldn't see him wince. The glow from the sun had long since gone. Aiden could barely see the man next to him.

Which was good, because Aiden couldn't stand this new silence between them.

"So, other than the twins, would anyone else notice that you've gone missing?" he asked. "You grew up in Willow Creek? I heard you Atwoods are pretty popular."

"Other than my friend Ray, no." Mack sounded strained. Aiden worried that he'd hit a nerve. He tried to make up for it.

"No other family or friends in town? Former classmates? A girlfriend?"

Aiden stopped himself when he realized he was fishing for information and not just making casual conversation.

But he also wanted to know the answer.

Mack Atwood was an interesting kind of mysterious. A reclusive bodyguard? Surely there was more to him than that.

So, Aiden waited.

And waited.

Finally, he turned to face Mack, ready to tell him that he could simply say he didn't want to answer instead of ignoring him. However, Aiden realized then that he'd been so focused on the wrong details that he had managed to glaze over some of the most pressing ones.

Mack was hurt.

He wasn't struggling for conversation. He was struggling to stay conscious.

Aiden watched as his silhouette slumped. Mack's head started to fall forward. It was a miracle Aiden was fast enough to catch him.

"Mack!"

The yell was useless.

The bodyguard was out.

Still, Aiden tried again.

"Mack?"

But there was no response.

THE FLOOR WAS tile and not at all cheap. Porcelain with several intricate designs placed every few feet. No design repeated. Several were multicolored, small squares that were rich in shades and hues that only the wealthy seemed to be able to afford, and some praised a single color only.

Every part of the floor shined.

The woman standing at the end of the foyer was no exception.

From her makeup and nails to shoes that cost more than most people's rent for an entire year, anyone looking her way would know that she was no mere mortal. She was money. She was power.

She could destroy him with a wave of her hand.

The downturn of her lips at the sight of him showed that she in fact was considering it.

He stopped on a circular design just out of her reach. The tiles were all blue. It reminded him of the angry clouds right before a storm. Maybe that's why she liked talking there. It set the tone. A subtle warning hidden in tile and grout.

He had to make sure it wasn't the last thing he saw.

He cleared his throat.

"Taking responsibility for what happened won't change that it happened," he started. "But I am fixing the problem I helped create. It will be resolved soon."

Her lipstick matched her shoes. It was hard to keep his eyes off both as she shifted her weight and spoke.

"I'm glad you've paid attention enough to know that people making excuses give me a migraine. But." Her voice had gone low. It was more intimidating that way. Sometimes he would have preferred it had she yelled. "People telling me they'll solve a problem instead of telling me they already have?" She tsked. "Well, it's less like a migraine and more like a sinus headache. One of those that builds and lets me know that in the near future I'm going to be downing ibuprofen and looking for a dark room."

Those perfectly manicured nails went to his collar in a flash. They wrapped the cloth into her fist and tightened his shirt around his neck.

"Money. Money can fix almost every problem in this world." Her voice was still hauntingly low. He kept eye contact, afraid if he looked away the attack would be more ferocious.

"*My* money?" she continued. "My money should have already taken Aiden out of his world and put him right here in ours."

She tightened her grip. He couldn't help but cough as it cut into his air supply for a moment.

She waited for him to get his composure back.

Then she let him go and straightened herself.

Her smile came back, but it was a twisted thing. There was no hidden threat there. It might as well have said in blinking neon lights that what she said next was her bottom line. And if he messed up, then he wouldn't be long for any of their worlds, money or not.

"I want Aiden," she started. "It's as simple as that. However, I don't need him. If he keeps making a fuss like he is, then I still want him, I just don't need the alive part. Understand?"

He knew he should just nod, but he had to vent his frustration.

"It's not Aiden that's the problem. It's that damn Atwood guy. Every chance we've taken, he's blocked it. If we could change the plan a little, we could get Aiden without anyone even—"

The slap was so fast that he never had a chance to react. One second he was looking at her and the next he was facing to the right, his gaze fallen to another intricate tile design on the floor.

This one had shades of violet.

"There is a reason I do what I do," she said. "If you want to make sure your friend keeps on living, then I suggest you think about getting rid of the Atwood problem. Not my plan. Or else I'll throw everything away and destroy you, Aiden and anyone else you've involved. Understood?"

He nodded.

"Understood."

He heard her heels click against the tile as she left the room.

Leighton didn't follow right away, because he knew as soon as he left the beautiful room that he would have to do something awful. It didn't feel right.

So, he stared at the tile a little longer.

Mack Atwood.

He wondered how hard it would be to kill him.

Chapter Twelve

He smelled smoke. Then he smelled rain. After that, he smelled oranges.

Mack opened his eyes and squinted against the light. It wasn't bright, but it was a shock all the same. Maybe not as much as what he saw when he adjusted to it.

He was no longer outside. No trees or mountain or a haunting memory standing sentry in the rain. He was in a room, a noisy one at that. Something was beeping, someone was whispering and farther away he could hear the sound of movement. The room was also warm. So was he. There was a blanket over him, tucked beneath his elbows. There was also a second, flannel one across the foot of the bed.

The bed.

It had rails, and he was propped up on two pillows.

It also had a tube. One that ran from his hand to the machines to his left.

The hospital.

He was in the hospital.

The whispering near him stopped.

Mack saw the two sitting on the couch under the window first, but the moment Ray saw him, he was up and moving. Goldie somehow managed to be faster. She was holding Mack's hand before Ray could reach the bed.

"I swear I'll go gray before I'm thirty with how much you make me stress, Malcolm Atwood." She shook her head. "I don't know what we should do with you."

She squeezed his hand. Her eyes were rimmed red. She had been crying.

Ray hadn't been, but he nodded with emphasis.

"It would be nice if you could live a less exciting life," he commented. "One that doesn't involve going to the hospital. I already work here. I don't like to visit here, too."

Mack wasn't sure how he had gotten there or what he had done to make them worry so much. In that moment, he only wanted to know one thing and one thing only.

"Where is he?" he rasped. "Where's Aiden?"

The last thing Mack remembered was sitting outside the warehouse. That was it.

Goldie shared a look with Ray. Ray smiled.

"He's in the room across the hall."

Mack tried to sit up more. He immediately regretted the decision. Pain bit at several parts of his body. His head also throbbed at the movement.

"Is he okay?"

Goldie and Ray both reached out to keep him from moving.

"Calm down there, cowboy," Ray said. "Don't worry, he's fine. Roughed up a bit, but he'll be good once he's had time to rest."

Relief temporarily pushed out Mack's pain.

"Not that you asked, but you *also* are okay," Ray added. The corner of his lips turned up. He pointed to Mack's head. "You have a concussion." He pointed at his own back. "Several gnarly bruises along your back, one that I'm guessing came from slamming into a tree, and—" Ray hovered both hands over his torso "—some superficial cuts along here. But the majority of your blood loss came from here."

Ray tapped the area around his chest.

Mack was confused.

"Blood loss?" He didn't remember that being an issue before he passed out. Twice.

Goldie was quick to answer. Mama Atwood couldn't hide the anger in it.

"You popped the stitches on your knife wound from your last job. I don't know how long you bled for, but Doc Ernest thinks it's one of the reasons you passed out when you did. By the time Ray and Aiden got back to you, your shirt was almost completely soaked in it."

Mack felt his eyebrows scrunch of their own accord. He was more interested in the Ray and Aiden of it than the fact that he had been slowly losing blood without realizing it.

"When you two got back?" he asked his friend. "What happened? How did you find us?"

Goldie and Ray shared another look. No words, but it was enough to come to a silent agreement. Goldie's eyes narrowed, and Ray nodded. He crossed his arms over his chest.

"It was complete luck, to be honest," he started. "I was heading to your place but going slow because of the rain. I don't think I would have seen him otherwise."

"Who?"

"Aiden," Goldie answered.

Ray nodded.

"He was running down the side of the road," he continued. "I recognized him from when he came to the morgue. I also knew he was supposed to be eating lunch with y'all. So when he started waving me down like a madman, I pulled over."

Mack grumbled.

"That was dangerous. He shouldn't have done that. It could have been someone else."

"He was trying to get you help," Goldie interjected. Mama Atwood's anger was coming back. "If he hadn't, who knows how long it would have been until you were found."

Mack decided it was smart not to respond.

"Anyway, as soon as I got him in the truck, we tore out there to get you and brought you in ourselves." Ray nodded to Goldie. "You've been out for about three hours."

Mack couldn't believe he'd passed out twice in one day. Or that he had lost three hours.

"What about the guys on the road?"

This time Ray's anger came out.

"Aiden gave as many details as he could remember about what happened, but we have no idea where your truck is or where they went after you two went down the mountain. The cowards seem to be good at hiding." His eyes widened. "Did you recognize them?"

Mack shook his head.

"I didn't get a great look at the driver of the car, but the man in the vest I'd never seen before."

"And you're sure they were after Aiden?" Goldie asked.

"Yeah. The second I had him out of the truck, they were running toward us." He could have explained more of the situation—Leighton, Bryce and Bellwether Tech—but Mack had more pressing matters.

"Has Detective Winters come yet?"

At this, Goldie bristled.

"He did. So did the sheriff."

"Aiden and I spoke to Winters," Ray said. "Goldie here handled the sheriff. Both lit off to try and find the guys.

Now we're all in a holding pattern. Speaking of, why don't you let Finn know Sleeping Beauty here is awake?"

"Finn's here, too?"

Goldie leveled a glare at him.

"Of course he is. You get yourself a ticket to the hospital and us three will always be in the audience. Those are the rules. Now, don't move too much. I'll be back in a bit. I'm also going to grab Doc Ernest and let her know you're up. No moving, okay?"

Mack thought better about saluting.

"Yes, ma'am, Mama Atwood. No moving for me."

Goldie snorted but seemed pleased with his response. She squeezed his hand one more time and left the room right after. Ray didn't budge from his spot. He lowered his voice.

"Really, though, how are you? I'm not going to lie, you looked pretty rough when we got to you."

"I'm fine." It was an automated response. He didn't like when others worried about him, and apparently that's all they had been doing for the last few hours.

Ray sighed. He rubbed a hand along the back of his neck.

"Goldie had no idea you were in trouble. Like, absolutely no idea. She thought you two had gone to Aiden's place or somewhere to lie low away from Sheriff Boyd and his favors. If Aiden hadn't left to try and get help, y'all would probably still be out there in this rain."

He glanced at the window. Mack did, too. The blinds were opened enough to see that the world outside was still dark and angry. When Ray's gaze slid back to Mack's, he seemed to be searching for the right words.

Mack waited until he had them.

"I don't know exactly what's going on or if Aiden is

someone to be trusted but, I will say this—he genuinely was worried about you," he finally said. "When he saw just how much you'd been bleeding, he seemed more upset than even me. He also refused to get seen in the ER until you were in a room. He actually got scolded by Scott, the doctor on call, for being stubborn." Ray grinned, but it fell just as fast. "I also heard them ask if he wanted to call anyone to stay with him, but he said there was no one. Not even his emergency contact would come if he asked. I don't know if he meant that to get sympathy or not, but it sure tugged at all of us. Finn and I have been taking turns hanging out with him since then."

That surprised Mack. Aiden seemed too social to have no one in his life.

"All his people must still be in Nashville," Mack reasoned. "Did he say who his emergency contact was?"

Ray's eyebrow popped up, but he didn't question it.

He shook his head instead.

"Whoever it is, I heard him say he needed to change it."

Mack wondered if it was his ex, Leighton.

"I was the one who was betrayed."

Aiden's confession in the woods only added to Mack's dislike for Leighton. He seemed to be nothing but a source of trouble. Then and now.

Mack motioned to himself.

"When can I leave?" he asked. It timed poorly with the door opening. Finn came in with a look that said that Mack definitely wasn't leaving any time soon.

"You can leave after rest and observation," Finn answered. "Neither of which you've cleared yet. So, hate to say it buddy, but you're here for a bit."

Mack grumbled.

Finn and Ray started to talk about how Mack was as fussy as a little kid at day care, wanting nothing more than to go home.

He didn't have the energy to tell them they were wrong.

He didn't want to go home.

He wanted to see Aiden.

THE HARPER FAITH HOSPITAL was small but, according to Finn, it was mighty. He chose to work there, in part, because of the great service and pristine conditions.

Aiden couldn't say he was wrong. So far he had been met with star treatment. Though, as the day stretched into late night, he started to suspect that was more because of the Atwoods than anything else. Goldie and Finn had revolved in and out of his room like clockwork until Aiden had finally convinced them, and Ray, that he was okay and wanted to be alone. They had all made sure that the doctor and nurses were aware that Aiden was someone they knew and they wanted him taken care of.

It had been touching and uncomfortable. Aiden wasn't used to that kind of attention.

Now, it was the middle of the night, and he found himself a little lonely. Maybe because he couldn't sleep. The wrap around his ribs was tight, and his ankle was in a temporary splint. Getting comfortable had been as much a battle as racing down the mountain. He was readjusting his pillows for the umpteenth time when a knock sounded on the door.

It was quiet.

Aiden looked at the clock on the wall. It was almost two in the morning.

"Come in?"

The door opened slowly. Mack walked in even slower. He was in a hospital gown and still hooked up to an IV pole.

"What are you doing up?" Aiden heard the scolding tone the same time as Mack.

He rolled his eyes.

"I just got Goldie off my back—I don't need you nagging me, too," he said. "This room is the same as mine, so who cares if I'm here or there? I'm a big boy."

He grumbled his way across the space and settled in the chair that Finn had been using. It was pushed up near the bed and put him close enough that Aiden helped hold the IV pole while Mack sat down. When he was settled, Mack swatted that hand away.

"Everyone keeps acting like I'm made of glass. I don't need any special handling. I'm fine."

Aiden narrowed his eyes.

"As someone who saw you being cut out of your clothes earlier in the ER, excuse me for still being a little concerned."

Mack seemed to consider that. A look of acute discomfort washed over him. He grumbled again, but there was no real weight to it.

"I don't like owing people, but I wanted to say thanks. You know, for getting me help and everything." Mack didn't look back to normal, but he definitely looked better than he had when they had rushed into the hospital lobby. Aiden was glad to see that his annoyance had resurfaced. "I'm not happy with how you went about it, but I can't complain about the results." Mack eyed his chest. "I guess we both needed some medical attention."

Aiden felt a flare of self-consciousness. He hadn't seen a mirror since he had been settled in his room but could only guess how awful he must look. Him being wrapped up like a mummy wasn't helping.

"If it wasn't for me, then you wouldn't have been in that situation," he pointed out. "It was the least I could do."

Mack looked like he wanted to say something but ended up nodding. Aiden's self-consciousness turned to guilt. In the past few days he'd gone from not knowing Mack Atwood to sharing a hospital room with him in the early hours of the morning.

To knowing his trauma.

Aiden's guilt was tenfold, and it was all thanks to Ray.

"It had to be here," Ray had said, staring through the windshield at the warehouse. The three of them had just gotten back to the truck. Aiden had been in the back seat holding the unconscious Mack, blood and rain mixing into their clothes.

Aiden could tell how upset Ray was for his friend but, in that moment, he had become distracted by what he was saying.

By the warehouse.

"Out of all the places in this town, he had to find here."

The comment sat for a few seconds before Ray went back to the task at hand and floored it to the hospital. It hadn't been until hours later when Ray had come in to say good night to Aiden that he had picked back up on the thought.

"Did Mack know y'all were heading to the warehouse when you were still on the mountain?" Ray had been sheepish.

Aiden had shaken his head.

"No. He thought we were going to Cayman's Loop."

Ray had looked pained at that.

"What did Mack say when he saw it was the warehouse?"

Originally, Aiden had wondered what the relationship was between Ray and Mack. It was obvious they were close. Ray made no issue about showing that fact, either, and, as far as Aiden could tell, Mack reciprocated that love.

If Aiden was being honest with himself, it had made him a little jealous. Ray talked a lot, just like Aiden, yet he doubted Ray got the look of annoyance as much as he did.

But, with Ray standing in his hospital room, almost sheepish, Aiden felt that the love for Mack was different. It felt more like Goldie and Finn's affection. Brotherly.

Aiden had answered truthfully to respect that bond.

"Cruel. He just said, 'Cruel.'"

Ray's face had fallen. He had opened his mouth, then closed it. Then opened it again.

"It's not my story to tell, but I'm not sure Mack can ever tell it. And I think you need to know why it is he can't let go of some things, even when they're dangerous."

Then Ray had come close to the hospital bed and told the story of why Mack Atwood hated the warehouse at the bottom of Willow Creek's only mountain.

"It used to be a storage-for-rent space for spillover product and equipment used mostly by companies out of Nashville for a cheap price. Nothing too fancy but popular enough that the contracts kept coming in. There was one client, though, who was a real pain. Always angry, rarely following the rules and eventually going as far as attacking the manager one day. No one really knows why the fight started, but when the sheriff's deputies showed, the client was told to leave. He wasn't happy about it and took his business elsewhere, though it suffered losses thanks to the bad attention. Then the fire broke out in the warehouse." He had paused there. It was like he'd aged twofold within the span of him talking. Just as Mack had aged after seeing the warehouse for the first time.

"The sprinkler system didn't go off, and the fire ate away at the office. There was so much smoke that most of downtown came when they saw it. A few of us even beat the fire trucks." He had sighed. "Mack was with me and we tried to help, but by the time we realized the manager was still trapped, it was too late. He didn't make it."

Aiden felt like he knew where the story was going. Still, he had to make sure.

"Who was the manager to Mack?"

Ray's frown had sunken in deep.

"His dad. It was his dad."

Cruel.

The comment had made sense then.

But that wasn't all.

"Mack has this thing with faces," Ray had continued. "He can meet someone only once and that's enough. From then on that face is stuck in his memory—even if someone ages or changes up their look, he can still almost always recognize them. That's why I believe him when he says he saw the client who caused trouble running from the warehouse the day of the fire, even though no one else does."

"What do you mean, no one believes him?"

Anger had taken over Ray's expression.

"The detective at the time chalked it up to grief. That Mack needed someone to blame, especially after the investigation was closed and the fire ruled an accident. But the rumor was that the client was let off because of a sob story about him being a dad with a kid who needed him and he really played up the story swell. Regardless of what happened, Mack stuck to his guns and didn't let it go. Even when everyone else did."

Ray had met Aiden's eye then.

"He's quiet, our Mack. He was before the fire and became quiet again after. But, when he was trying to get justice for his father, he became loud. Angry. Someone who didn't give up and never gave in. If it wasn't for the twins begging him to try and move on and live his life, I'm not sure where Mack would be now. But one thing I *do* know is whatever is going on with you, with those guys, he's angry about it. And, quiet or not, he's going to see it through. If not for you, for the mere fact that they did the one thing everyone in this town knows not to do when it comes to Mack Atwood." He hadn't paused for dramatic effect, but Aiden had felt goose bumps crawl along his arms at Ray's next words. "They reminded Mack what it felt like to be loud."

Now, that man was sitting next to him, simply trying to get comfortable in a chair.

Aiden made a decision.

It was time to tell a story.

Aiden cleared his throat.

"I found out a secret about Bellwether Tech, and I think it's worth killing for."

Chapter Thirteen

"Bellwether Tech isn't original. They didn't break the mold with their security system or their programming. All they did was promote it differently than what was on the market at the time."

Mack watched Aiden squirm a little. He wasn't sure if it was because of the topic at hand or if his injuries were still bothering him. Without a gown covering Aiden's top half Mack could see that most of the man's torso and chest were wrapped up. He knew from experience how uncomformable that could be.

If he wasn't invested in what Aiden was saying, he would have let his anger roll around some more unchecked.

Instead he leaned in when Aiden asked him a question.

"Do you know what Bellwether does? I mean, what their main product is."

Mack hadn't known before meeting Aiden, but afterward he'd done some light research.

"The Sitter. It's a home security system with cameras and alarms."

Aiden nodded.

"Instead of competing with other home security systems for people at home, it was marketed as a system that worked as a house sitter for those who were away from the home. Specifically for people who traveled a lot or were deployed. Not really revolutionary, but then the system went viral after a service member who was deployed in Germany was able to see that his home was being broken into. From there he was able to coordinate in real time with the local authorities to catch the guys, who were trying to make off with his late wife's jewelry collection. Something that obviously meant a lot to the man."

"I actually remember that story," Mack said. "It was on the news with the guy tearing up about almost losing what he had left to remember her by. I didn't realize that was connected to Bellwether."

"That story is what really made the company go boom and also made it a fan favorite of veterans and service members. Last I checked, nearly 75 percent of users were deployed. The company also took advantage of the popularity and offered discounts specific to those in the military, too."

Aiden took a deep breath. When he let it out, his body dragged down a little with it.

"When I joined the company, it was at the height of their popularity. It was a low-level job that I was overqualified for. They'd just gone through several rounds of hiring to meet their new demands and I'd missed out. Still, I liked Nashville and wanted to work for them, so I didn't mind doing grunt work for a while. That's when I met Leighton Hughes."

Mack wanted to grumble at the name. He didn't. Aiden kept on.

"He was big in the IT department and well respected by the higher-ups, especially the owner. We became friends after meeting in the company cafeteria and started eating lunch together every day. We talked about work at first, and then one day we were talking about each other. Somehow after that we were dating." A brief smile passed over Aiden's lips. Mack shifted his weight in his chair. "We were together when an upgrade to the Sitter went live. And broke everything in our system. I mean, catastrophically broke. Everyone was rushing into the office at three in the morning in their pajamas trying to fix it. It was chaos. I was driving Leighton in while he had his laptop up in the passenger's seat and his phone *and* my phone both on speaker. By the time we got to the office, no one had a workable solution."

The way he said *no one* gave Mack the impression that there was, in fact, one person who had.

"No one except you, I'm guessing," he said.

"I got lucky," Aiden admitted. "I found the problem and had it fixed within five minutes. But, after that, I was promoted to the lead IT team." Aiden's smile was quick again. There was pride in it. Strangely, Mack felt it, too. "Alongside Leighton, I was invited into the inner circle of the higher-ups with the new job. Wining and dining, fancy events—you name it and I had a pass to be there. I was trusted."

There was no more pride. No more smiles. Aiden seemed to fold in on himself.

"So I didn't question it when I was called in to the office late one night. We'd just done a minor update, so I thought I was there to fix something with that. Instead they presented me with a special project, one that they didn't want getting out. At first, I didn't question that, either. I think some of that was my ego getting the best of me. After working my butt off in college and through part-time jobs, I finally was being acknowledged and praised for my skills." He sighed. "Then I saw what they wanted me to do."

Aiden stopped. Like he'd run into a verbal brick wall. When he didn't start again, Mack reached out. It was as easy as breathing. He placed his hand on top of Aiden's. The new weight seemed to focus the man again.

Then there were trees in the room between them. Green eyes searching Mack's.

"I don't have to tell you," Aiden said. It wasn't a statement of defiance but an offering. Mack patted Aiden's hand.

"I want to know."

"Are you sure?"

Mack was. He nodded.

"Tell me."

Aiden held his gaze a little longer. Then he shared his secret.

"They wanted me to hack into a specific home's live feed, cut it off and loop it with preexisting footage. And they needed me to do it in under one minute." His defeat turned to anger. "I was told that it was a test. A way to see if hackers could infiltrate the system and manipulate the program. I should have asked more questions, but I was so excited to have a new challenge, so I did it. Fifty-four seconds. That's all it took."

Aiden's fist balled beneath Mack's hand.

"But then Leighton started acting weird, and I couldn't let the feeling go that I'd done something wrong," he continued. "So, I went a little overboard. I hacked into our secure server…and then the personal computers of the vice president and CEO."

Mack felt his eyes widen.

Aiden nodded.

"I know, I know. I went from one extreme to the other, but when I was in Bellwether's security logs I kept finding the vice president's digital prints everywhere. Then when I went into his computer, I found a digital calendar with customer names pinned at odd times. I couldn't figure out why, and so I went to the CEO's personal network after finding a message chain between them about a video file the CEO wanted destroyed." His words had sped up and were almost crashing into each other now. "From there I found two videos in the trash that hadn't actually been completely deleted, restored them and realized I was looking at previous live footage from a customer's home. In the video the man was meeting up with a woman—a woman who was not his wife. I then went back to Bellwether Tech's storage and realized that every trace of the video had been deleted and in its place, with a fabricated time stamp, was a looped video from a previous recording."

Aiden had to stop to catch his breath.

Once done, he was full speed again.

"Then I looked into the CEO's personal finances and found a transaction for $50,000 that had been transferred the day before the footage had been changed and deleted. That got me curious about who paid it, and I realized it was the customer from the video. From there I was able to find security footage that showed the vice president and the customer meeting in the parking garage, the customer looking absolutely furious. I kind of figured out what happened from there."

"Your company used a home's footage from the Sitter to blackmail a customer," Mack laid out.

Aiden was defeated.

"And I had helped them get into another home's live footage and loop it after that."

"What did they do with that customer? Did you figure it out?"

Aiden shook his head.

"Instead of investigating by hacking absolutely everyone, I decided to confide in someone I trusted in the company to hopefully get some help. That was a mistake."

"I was the one betrayed."

Mack recalled Aiden's earlier confession in the woods. This was where Leighton Hughes came in.

"I told Leighton everything I knew and asked him to come to the police with me." Mack felt Aiden's fist tighten beneath his hand again. "But Leighton convinced me to let him figure out what was really going on first. And I, well, I believed in Leighton's judgment. I believed in him."

There was that wall again. Aiden skidded into it and stopped talking altogether.

This time Mack waited for him to find his words on his own.

After a few moments, he did.

"A couple of days later Leighton told me he'd handled it and nothing like that would ever happen again. I expected a resignation or a change in management, but nothing happened. When I confronted Leighton about it, he told me that the CEO and vice president had apologized profusely and given the money back. I wanted to check if that was true, but Leighton…he lost it. He told me if I ever loved him that I'd drop it, leave well enough alone. And so I did. I quit the next day and never went back. Leighton and I tried to stay together, treating what happened like it was some kind of professional experience only, but I couldn't get over the fact that he was okay with everything. That he still was working there, still attending the parties, still rubbing all the elbows. So, I ended things there, too. Six months later, here I am."

Mack could tell the story was through by his body language alone. He looked relieved and tired all at once. Mack felt for him. Maybe too much. He pulled his hand away and straightened his back.

"Did anyone else know about what happened? Did Bryce Anderson?"

Aiden shook his head.

"I didn't tell anyone. Only Leighton. I wasn't even there when he confronted the vice president and CEO. When I resigned, Leighton handled that himself. I told everyone else I was leaving for personal reasons. No one asked past that. That's why I want to find Leighton so badly, too. He's the only one who can answer at least half of my questions."

"But he hasn't gotten back in touch with you since the message he left with Mrs. Cole," Mack finished.

"Yeah. And I really do think the email came from him, too."

Aiden's eyes widened.

"The email that was sent from an address here in Willow Creek. The same one I still haven't been able to check. Every time I'm headed that way, someone tries to grab me."

He said it in a mocking way, as if it was a small inconvenience, but Mack saw some discomfort at the memories. It didn't help that they were in the hospital after the most recent attack.

Aiden hung his head low. One of the bruises along his jaw was a sickening purple.

"I know I could go to the police about what happened at Bellwether Tech, but now I'm afraid if I do that it might somehow put Leighton's life in danger. I also know he's my ex and I shouldn't be worried like this but, he was a good guy once. Until I know he's not now, it's hard to ignore that fear."

Aiden kept his head down. His hand, however, reached out. It wrapped around Mack's.

"If you were me, what would you do?"

The touch, the question, the way Aiden's voice wavered during both, made Mack tense. Adrenaline surged, his breath quickened in response. Suddenly the fluorescent lights overhead became louder. The machines beeping, gunshots. Mack's heartbeat, fireworks in a calm night sky. His mind raced along with the changes.

His mouth formed the words before he realized what he was saying.

"You're smart. You don't need to know what I would do. Trust yourself." Aiden's hand was smaller than his, but it warmed his easily. *"But—"*

Aiden raised his chin.

"But?" he repeated.

The trees were back. Mack stared into them.

"But, whatever you decide, I'll be right there with you."

Aiden's eyebrow rose sky-high.

"You've already done enough," he tried.

"As a friend, maybe. But not as a part of my job."

"Your job?" Aiden repeated.

Mack smirked.

"Congratulations, Mr. Riggs, I'm officially your new bodyguard."

HARPER FAITH HOSPITAL was nice and all, but Aiden preferred seeing it in the rearview mirror.

"I know we were in there for only two days, but I'm very, very happy we're going in the opposite direction."

His back seat buddy, Mack the Bodyguard, snorted. Their driver, Finn, laughed.

"I don't know who complained more about his stay," he said. "You or big bro there. I thought Goldie was going to lose it on you two when you tried sneaking out after day one."

Aiden and Mack shared a look. Mack played it cool; Aiden's cheeks heated a little. True enough, the morning after they had talked in his room, they had tried to get discharged early. Goldie had appeared like magic before either could go through the process. Aiden thought if anyone could get around her, it would be Mack, but after she had pulled him into another room and given him a thorough talking-to, he'd come back like a dog with his tail tucked between his legs.

"Let's just wait until the doc says we can go," he had said, like it was his idea first.

Aiden had listened, though that had less to do with being reasonable as Goldie had said and more to do with what Mack had agreed to do.

He was now Aiden's bodyguard.

Aiden would have been less surprised if Mack had admitted to being close personal friends with Dolly Parton.

When he had told Mack his story, he hadn't been fishing for sympathy or pity. He had wanted to give Mack context for what he'd gone through. Though Aiden also knew sharing the secret wasn't entirely selfless.

It had felt good—more than good—to share his regret. His worry. His shame. Not only in him walking away from a problem he knew existed but for how he had found that problem out in the first place.

He'd broken several laws and done the one thing he had told himself he wouldn't do again once he was an adult.

No more hacking.

No more peeking behind the curtain.

But, once he'd looked, he hadn't been able to stop himself.

It was like an addiction.

An addiction that he'd admitted to one person and one person only.

Aiden could feel Mack's body heat against his leg. Finn's car was on the small side, and the front and back seats were filled with work materials. Aiden had thought Mack would make a fuss at having to scrunch into the back seat, but he hadn't. Instead he had asked Aiden several times if he was sure he wasn't in any pain once they were seated.

He was, just a bit, but moving to the front passenger seat wasn't going to change that.

Willow Creek always had some housing turnover, according to Aiden's Realtor, simply because of time. People grew older, left homes, got new jobs, fell in love and passed away. All those reasons were why he had been able to buy 142 Lockley Way. One story, wrapped in whitewashed brick and absolutely spacious compared to his last apartment, the house was an oasis spaced between elderly neighbors and a new family with two babies. None of these neighbors were outside as Finn parked at the curb.

Aiden was surprised to see a truck in the driveway.

"It's mine," Mack said, answering his unasked question. "Your car is still at my place. We can get it later."

Aiden felt a little heat crawl up into his cheeks again. He had gotten into the habit of feeling out of the loop when he was with Atwood and Company. Even though apparently he was in the center of their attention the last few days.

"You know, you really don't have to do this." It wasn't the first time he had said it.

It also wasn't the first time Mack had waved him off.

"There's no going back now. I'm already on the clock." He opened the car door but paused to talk over the seat to Finn. "I'll keep you updated. Let me know when you get home."

Finn saluted over his shoulder.

"Yes, sir. You have all our numbers in your new phone, right?"

"Sure do, Wonder Twin. Thanks for the ride."

Mack was quick for a man with two sets of stitches and a patch quilt of bruises. He was out of the vehicle before Aiden could finish unbuckling. He disappeared behind the car and opened the trunk.

Finn redirected his attention to Aiden.

"Since they found your phone on the mountain and you have our numbers, we expect you to call or text if you need anything. That's me, Goldie and Ray. Anytime, any day."

Aiden smiled. He was as touched as he had been when the three of them had taken his phone from Deputy McCoy's hand at the hospital and passed it around to put their numbers in.

"I will," he promised.

Finn nodded. Then his eyes softened.

"I know Mack is strong, but sometimes it's the strong ones who need the most from the rest of us," he said, voice lowered. "Watch his back while he watches yours. Okay?"

Aiden didn't have time to answer, but maybe it wasn't needed. Finn's attention went back to the front of the car as Mack appeared at the opened door. He held his hand out and down. Aiden took it and was guided outside with obvious care.

"You know, I'm also not made of glass," he deadpanned

to Mack. "The doctor even said he was surprised at how resilient my body is to pain."

Mack snorted.

"I'm not sure that's something you should brag about." He thumped the roof of the car. Finn took it as his sign to leave. He was no sooner out of the driveway than Aiden realized what Mack had taken from the trunk.

"What's in the duffel?" Aiden asked. It was different from the one he'd had at the hospital the last two days.

"It's my go bag. Clothes, toiletries, a few tools of the trade."

Aiden cocked his head.

"And why do you need a go bag?" He laughed. "Are you an undercover spy who's just been found out by some kind of tyrannical mob boss? Please tell me your passport isn't in there."

Mack rolled his eyes.

"I definitely can tell you feel better based on how much you've been talking today. You could almost give Finn a run for his money."

He said it like he was annoyed, but Aiden didn't feel it like he had when they had first met. He wondered if that's how Mack operated as a bodyguard. Instead of lurking in the shadows, ready for anything, like Aiden had pictured, maybe the oldest Atwood was more hands-on.

The thought stirred something in Aiden, but he focused on the conversation at hand.

"Seriously, though, why the bag?" he asked. "Aren't you just here to take a look at my house and then bring me back to my car at yours?"

Mack snorted this time. He grabbed the sleeve of Aiden's

shirt and pulled it and Aiden along with him toward the front porch.

"I hate to break it to you but, until we get to the bottom of this, I'm not leaving your side."

Aiden's heartbeat picked up a little at that.

"What about tonight?" They hadn't explicitly laid out any plan, let alone sleeping arrangements.

Mack answered like it was no big deal.

"Day or night, wherever you are, I'm going to be right there next to you."

Chapter Fourteen

What Aiden didn't know was that Mack had already scouted his house before they had even left the hospital. It wasn't that he was trying to keep secrets from the man, it had just been a matter of efficiency.

"You guessed right," Ray had said once the task had been done. "Aiden's one of those trusting types who hides his spare key in the flower bed. I found it under a fake rock."

At the time of the call, Mack had been in the hallway outside said man's hospital room. He'd had the urge to go inside to scold him about having better safety measures. Instead they had used the breach in security to send Ray and Finn inside to make sure there was nothing or no one lying in wait.

It was usually a task that Mack would have carried out, but leaving Aiden alone wasn't an option anymore. So, he'd listened as his best friend and brother more or less broke into Aiden's house, all in the name of safety.

Thankfully, there was nothing too alarming.

"Other than the most tricked-out home office I've ever seen, I don't think anyone has been inside here doing anything bad," Ray had concluded once they had finishing sweeping the place. "I think it's fine to bring him here for now. Though, if he's being targeted, location might not matter if they're eager."

Mack knew this, just as he knew the house had been fine an hour earlier. It's why he put himself between Aiden and every room after they went inside. It's also why he had his Taser and baton in the bag across his shoulder. He wasn't a fan of guns, but he had no qualms about using anything else to defend his client.

Client.

Mack watched as Aiden peeked around the door into his office.

"I'm glad Mrs. Cole conditioned me to clean up after pulling all-nighters or else this room would look like a frat house after-party. Empty cans, food wrappers and random underwear hanging off the ceiling fan." Aiden made himself laugh. Some of his hair fell at the movement, brushing into his eyes.

Normally this would be when Mack repeated the word *client*. Reminding himself that he was there to keep someone safe, not joke around. Not chat. Not look at simply for the sight.

Yet, the word that came to mind wasn't *client*. It had nothing to do with a job.

Handsome.

Aiden Riggs was handsome.

There wasn't a specific thing about him that Mack liked. It wasn't his high cheekbones, his full lips, the mole near his green eyes or the dimples that came out when he smiled. It wasn't his earring or his clothes that always seemed to have some kind of stylish black piece. It wasn't his lean frame or the fact that they had an intriguing height difference between them.

It wasn't just any one thing, he realized.

Mack liked all of it.

But the thing he liked the most had nothing to do with the man's looks.

Aiden just kept going.

Talking, laughing, smiling, worrying, caring, joking. He just kept on no matter what had happened. No matter that his body was broken and bruised, no matter that he was scared and angry and confused.

At first Mack had preferred being alone. Then he hadn't disliked being around Aiden. Now he was standing in his house and wanting to know more about him.

Also wanting to tuck his hair behind his ear.

Mack flexed his hand. He cleared his throat and instead nodded to the computer setup that Ray had already commented on.

"I doubt a frat party would have something like this going on. I know I'm more of an analog guy, but surely this isn't normal."

The room was on the small size, but Aiden had utilized all the space well. A long desk stretched along the back wall and had two tiers of shelving at the top. Then there were three monitors, all mounted on the wall with what looked like adjustable rods. Mack spied at least four keyboards, two of which had multicolored LED lights along them, and there were several gadgets and cute trinkets holding pens, pencils and sticky notes. Mack eyed a pair of headphones displayed near the center monitor.

"That definitely isn't something I think I'd see at a frat party," he added.

Aiden scoffed and brushed past him. He picked up the

headphones and slipped them on. They were silver and white. They also were shaped like cat ears.

"I'll have you know that these are trendy, thank you very much. And look, you can do this, too." He reached up and clicked a button. The cat ears lit up. Aiden smiled wide. "Let me guess, you have some no-nonsense things at home. I bet they're earbuds. And you only wear them when you're mowing the lawn or something."

Mack pulled out his cell phone.

Aiden was still waiting for an answer to his teasing.

Mack took a picture instead.

"Hey, now." Aiden reached out for the phone. Mack took an easy step away from his grasp.

"As your bodyguard, I need a current photo of you just in case," Mack explained.

"Not of me in cat ears!" Aiden took the headphones off, but the damage was done.

"I'll make that call. I'm the professional here, after all."

Aiden kept fussing. Mack expected him to keep going longer, maybe even trying to swipe at him a few more times, but the man's expression changed. It was like he put on a mask. His smile melted. What was left was a seriousness that made Mack straighten.

"Will you really follow me anywhere?" he asked. "As my bodyguard?"

Mack nodded. "Within reason," he amended. "I won't let you put yourself in danger willingly, if that's what you're asking."

"What if I'm not entirely sure if a place is safe or not?"

Mack's eyebrow rose in question.

Aiden reached into his pocket. He pulled out a sticky note and handed it over. It was an address. The same one they had been on the way to visit before they had been stopped by the men on the road.

"I know the sheriff's department is looking into Leighton being missing, where your truck is, who those guys were and where they went, plus who killed Bryce, but I never told Detective Winters about this." Aiden shrugged to himself. "I don't know why I didn't but, well, I didn't. Now, I want to still keep it from him because *I* want to see what's there first. And I want you to be there with me. What do you say?"

Mack should have said no—he should have said let law enforcement know they might have a lead—but he didn't.

"Are you sure you're up for it?"

Aiden didn't miss a beat.

"With you by my side, why wouldn't I be?"

THE WEATHER WAS NICE. The sun was out, a breeze kept coming and going and there was something blooming nearby that smelled like heaven. Willow Creek wasn't all bad. Minus the murder, road traps and mountains soaked in rain, Aiden was reminded why he'd picked the scenic little town to settle down in.

It had a charm to it. A cinematic filter that made the buildings, fields and good number of trees charming and warm.

He nodded to himself, still happy with his decision to open Riggs Consulting. Nashville wasn't bad, but Willow Creek felt more like his speed.

Again, minus the murder and mayhem.

"How many pain meds did you take?"

Aiden turned his head from the window and looked long at his driver.

Mack had one hand slung on the steering wheel and the other resting on the gearshift. It was automatic, not manual, and not needed, but the stance screamed smooth. So did the jeans, the black tee and the flannel button-up left open wide. Never mind the man's obvious good looks. He bet if he told Mack how attractive he was, Mack would snort and say he was talking too much. Then, since Aiden had grown fond of annoying the man, he would have come back and said something about how anyone talked more than the wall that was him.

But, since Aiden was genuinely curious about what Mack had asked, he delayed that urge.

"Excuse me?"

Mack smirked.

"I'm wondering if you snuck some extra pain meds before we left the house. You're humming."

"I was humming?"

"Mmm-hmm."

Aiden was taken slightly aback by that.

"I guess I was in the zone."

He motioned toward the scenery they were currently passing. It was a small field on the far side of town, in the opposite direction of downtown and in one of the few areas of town that Aiden hadn't actually visited before. Mack said he knew where the address was located but also hadn't visited the area. At least not in the last ten years or so.

"I usually don't get out to enjoy nice weather like this," Aiden added. "Forgetting to go outside can be a hazard of the job sometimes. It wasn't until Mrs. Cole got friendly that she and her husband started forcing me outside on occasion. She sometimes calls me her potted plant. She's afraid that if she forgets to give me sunlight, I'll wither."

"You have a Mrs. Cole, I have a Goldie," Mack mused. "Though I'm not a vampire like you. She worries that I don't eat enough." His big hand made a thud against his stomach for emphasis. "I don't know why. I think I'm pretty sturdy as it is."

Aiden's gaze betrayed him and cut down to Mack's torso. Then it had the audacity to slide slowly up his chest. That black tee sure did fit nice.

"My eyes are up here, Potted Plant."

If Aiden had been the one driving, he would have wrecked them out at that. Mack's easy blues met his stare with a knowing look. Aiden's cheeks felt like fire.

"You're the one who slapped yourself and got my attention," he defended. "I'm not a potted plant *or* a vampire. I'm just a genius hacker who has a problem with hyperfocus and sleep schedules. I think that's pretty typical in my line of work."

Mack's eyes went back to the road ahead. He put his blinker on as they got closer to a small intersection. It had seen better days. No one was around in any direction, either.

"I don't think you're typical," Mack said after a moment. "I don't know about genius, though. Aren't they usually not so self-aware to claim that about themselves?"

Aiden rolled his eyes.

"Tell me your favorite color, the first job you ever had and your childhood best friend's name and I can have your Social Security number within ten minutes. Ten minutes after that and I'll know everything about Malcolm Atwood. A few minutes more and I could destroy you if I wanted, easy. If that's not genius, then give it another name."

Mack was quick.

"Stalker."

Aiden mocked offense. Too well. He slapped his hand against his chest to be dramatic. But he forgot he was actually hurt. Pain radiated from the hit. He winced. The truck slowed; Mack's concern did not.

"Are you okay?" He reached over like a mom trying to use her arm as a seat belt after having to slam on the brakes. Aiden sucked in a breath and nodded into an embarrassed laugh.

"I forgot that I fell down a mountain." He patted Mack's arm. "I'm good. Sorry for the scare."

Mack shook his head.

"This is why you need a bodyguard. I can't trust you by yourself."

There Aiden went again with his blush.

"You sure know how to make a client feel special." He swatted Mack's hand that was still hovering away. "I bet your girlfriend sure likes that sweet-talking."

It was another casual girlfriend comment, a way to try and annoy Mack. Yet Aiden would be lying if he said he didn't hold his breath a little waiting for a response.

And he sure got one.

Just not one he wanted.

"That's the address up ahead."

Aiden whipped his attention back to the windshield. They were driving along a narrow street, trees back on each side. Ahead of them was a two-story house. It had blue shutters, a tin roof and a hand-painted sign that hung from the mailbox. Aiden couldn't read it until they were parking at the curb next to it.

"'Bluebird Breeze,'" he read aloud. "This also sounds like a really bad name for a club."

Mack peered out past the sign to the house.

"I think it's a vacation rental." He pointed to the side of the house. "There are Realtor locks on the garage and front door. No cars in the driveway, either."

"I didn't know there were rental properties here in Willow Creek."

Mack nodded.

"Goldie said they've gotten more popular. There's a few in the new neighborhoods. I didn't think there would be one out here. Last time I was out this way, the De Lucas lived here. There's no way that Mr. De Luca would let anyone name his home, former or current, after a bird, though."

"If this is a rental then maybe Leighton is staying here. Or was." Aiden didn't understand why Leighton would be at a rental in town without letting him know ahead of time. At least not why he would be there only to send an email and not come see Aiden in person. Riggs Consulting was downtown, but it wasn't that far. "Let's go," Aiden added.

He had no idea what they would find, but he was ready to look.

Mack must have been on the same wavelength.

"Let's go, then." He unbuckled his seat belt and then surprised Aiden by reaching across him for his buckle. Aiden froze as it came undone.

That cold thawed in an instant when Mack sat back in his seat.

"And, by the way, I don't have a girlfriend."

Then that bodyguard went and exited the car like he hadn't just set Aiden on fire.

Chapter Fifteen

No one was home. All the doors were locked, no sound or movement came from inside, and the number on the Bluebird Breeze sign went to an automated voice mail recording.

"I don't know what I expected, but this is disappointing." Aiden was peering through a window over the front porch. Mack could hear that disappointment with ease. Even though he didn't want to deal with Aiden's ex, he was also put off by their lead not going anywhere.

"We'll just have to get in touch with the owner and see if they can tell us who booked this place," Mack reasoned. He left off the fact that he preferred this safer option over potentially running into more trouble.

Aiden sighed.

"This won't do." Aiden walked past Mack and to the truck with purpose. He opened the back door and set up his bag on the seat. "We tried the usual way to get our information. Now we're going to try the impatient way."

Mack looked over the man's shoulder as he pulled out his laptop and powered it on. It didn't look as high-tech as the computers in Aiden's home office, but the thing responded to his touch faster than Mack's phone had ever worked for him.

"What are you doing?"

Aiden's fingers were lightning across the keys, and not for one second did his gaze seem to track their movements. Working with computers really was second nature for him. All Mack could do was watch as different windows popped up on the screen and were filled with words and code he didn't understand.

"Bluebird Breeze is listed on a rental website," Aiden said after a moment. "It's not a big-name website, though. It looks like it might be local to a realty place in Knoxville, not Nashville. Not that that means much, but I always feel more comfortable digging in someone else's sandbox when said sandbox is at least an hour or two away from me."

His clicking and typing accelerated. Mack became worried.

"Wait. What do you mean, digging in someone else's sandbox? What exactly are you doing?"

Aiden didn't break his stride.

"I can tell you now or when I'm done. I'll let you decide which is better for your grumpiness levels."

Mack rubbed along his jaw.

"What's the difference in you telling me now or when you're done if you still tell me?"

Aiden stopped for a moment to read something on the screen. Mack couldn't have deciphered it had you begged him.

"If I tell you now, you might feel inclined to stop me, and I'm not in the mood to do that," Aiden explained. "This will only make me sarcastic and want to fight you. Then you'll undoubtedly get grumpy, which will only make *me* grumpy and suddenly we're back in the truck not talking while a murder mystery and an unknown group of guys makes our lives miserable. *But*, if you wait until I'm done, all you can do is scold me with some kind of life lesson. And I won't fault you for that, because I'm sure I can use more of those."

He delivered the whole speech almost within one breath. Mack would have been impressed if he hadn't had to make a choice.

"You'd lose in a fight against me," he pointed out. "So just tell me when you're done."

He expected Aiden to say something snappy, but the computer whiz was all in on the task at hand. Since Mack didn't understand what was happening on the screen, he lowered his chin and stared down at the man typing.

Aiden was a man possessed. The focus was unlike any Mack had seen from him. His jaw was clenched, his eyes narrowed yet constantly shifting. There was a crease between his brows. One that, even in profile, was severe. The corners of his lips downturned and deepened. He could have been searching Google for a pound cake recipe, stealing nuclear launch codes or erasing every trace of Mack's life online...and Mack would have kept on staring.

Aiden Riggs was back in his element and, for the life of him, Mack couldn't look away.

For years Mack had spent his career protecting people. Business tycoons, children of important people, the wealthy, the unfortunate, the paranoid. He had spent countless hours standing in rooms, in hallways, sitting in cars, walking in darkness, scanning faces and watching shadows. He had met people so completely opposite him, so eerily similar and all temperaments in between. People who had achieved greatness, people who were aiming higher. People who wanted to be just like everyone else. People who never could be.

Mack had felt like he had met every kind of person, seen every kind of marvel on the job. However, watching Aiden use a laptop in the back seat of his truck, not understanding a thing he was doing, had Mack transfixed.

I like this, he realized.

Then, within another breath, he realized something else. *I like him.*

That was it. Aiden wasn't a rich socialite with a secret. He wasn't the son of a CEO at war with his rivals. He hadn't created a new drug that would revolutionize the world. He probably wouldn't ever change even part of the world.

Yet, with almost no effort, he had gone and changed Mack's.

It didn't make sense. There was no logic to it. He was just a man who had spent a week meeting bad luck at Mack's side.

But there it was.

Mack liked Aiden. He liked that he talked too much. He liked that he was annoying. He liked his clothes and his earring. He liked how he was short and had eyes that reminded him of trees. He liked that his family and Ray had fallen into step alongside him. He liked that he was obviously smart but didn't really push it home. He liked that he'd chased down a guy who had just attacked him, trying to help Mack. He liked that, even though Mack had been rude to him, that he'd still stood up for him against Detective Winters's snide comments.

He liked that Aiden had asked if he had a girlfriend.

And maybe the most telling thing was that Mack had liked telling him that he didn't.

Mack liking men wasn't the part that had him surprised—he had always liked men. It was the actually wanting to date someone, to be with someone, feeling that had been absent. Now, though, was the strange part. In the most opposite of romantic settings, he was having such an epiphany about himself. He wanted more, finally, and Mack wasn't mad about it.

"I married your mom despite her entire family being against it. The hassle of us dating was enough to make any hero in a romance movie run for the hills. But, you know what, son? I have a rule about the heart. If people say your love doesn't have a place in this world, the most fun thing you can do is prove them wrong by carving out your own little island for it. What's more fun than waving at angry people on shore from your own slice of paradise?"

His father's words had been imprinted in his memory like every face Mack had ever seen. It helped that he and the twins had grown up hearing the ill-fated love story between their parents every time one of them got wistful. Even though eventually their grandparents had softened and accepted their father.

Goldie had particularly liked the image of sunbathing on a beach, hand in hand with the love of your life while smiling slyly at a bunch of people miserable behind their binoculars on a dirt-covered shore.

That was too flowery for Mack, but he took the lesson to heart.

Like who you like. Love who you love. Don't fight it. Live better than those who want to try.

The sound of clicking keys penetrated Mack's trip down memory lane and brought him back to the present.

He liked Aiden, and he accepted that. But it didn't mean he was going to act on it.

They weren't on an island. They were in Willow Creek,

and someone in town wanted Aiden. Until they could figure out who and why, Mack couldn't let himself be distracted.

The knife wound on his side seemed to wake up long enough to agree. He had been distracted by something trivial on his last job and had wound up in the hospital. If he gave in to something like his feelings?

Well, Mack didn't want another trip to the hospital, or worse, for Aiden.

So, he decided to stay quiet. To push everything down and focus on the task at hand.

A task that Aiden had finished. He pointed at the laptop screen with enthusiasm.

"And that's why I'm amazing," he exclaimed.

Mack cleared his throat.

"Does that mean it's time for you to explain it to me?"

Aiden laughed and nodded.

Then he became serious.

"So most of these smaller businesses have a habit of being a little lazy with their reservation systems. I found the last three guests who rented this place. The last one made a reservation a month ago, and it showed her checking in last week. See? Right here." He highlighted a line of text. "It was made under the name Taliyah Smith."

He turned to face Mack, eyebrow raised.

"I thought it would be Leighton. I don't know a Taliyah Smith."

Mack gritted his teeth.

"But I do." Aiden's eyebrow rose higher. Mack wasn't sure his answer was going to make that confusion go away. "Taliyah Smith is Jonathan Smith's sister."

Aiden's eyes widened.

"Jonathan Smith, as in—"

"—as in the man who attacked you in your car the night we met."

AIDEN WAS RIDING a new adrenaline surge.

It made watching Mack pace next to the truck while on the phone that much more frustrating. He wanted some action. He wanted some progress. Instead all he could do was tap his foot and wait.

Not that that did him any good. Mack ended his call and sighed his way over.

"Jonathan is in the county jail but, before that, he'd been staying with his ex-girlfriend over on Mockingbird Drive. That's on the other side of town. The sheriff's department confirmed the story. At least, that's what Goldie found out."

Aiden crossed his hands over his chest. It hurt a little, but his confusion outweighed it.

"What about his sister, Taliyah?"

Mack shook his head.

"The reservation might be under her name, but she's with their dad out of the country. Has been for almost two weeks."

Aiden swung around and gave the Bluebird Breeze a deadly stare.

"So there's no reason for Taliyah to reserve this place, and there was no reason for her brother to stay here." He grumbled out sounds of frustration. He felt Mack's presence as the bodyguard stopped at his side. Normally the one to grumble, he was more graceful with his.

"Is there any connection between Leighton and Jonathan?"

The thought had already crossed his mind. Aiden had to shrug.

"As far as I know, I don't think so. Then again, other than a few phone calls and messages, I haven't exactly kept close tabs on Leighton since we broke up."

"Maybe Leighton was never here."

It was such a startlingly simple statement that Aiden caught himself gaping at the man. Mack met his look with an even one.

"You might not know where Leighton is, but the fact is, you've never known where he was." Mack nodded to the house. "Just because we know Bryce Anderson couldn't have sent the email about Bellwether Tech to you from here doesn't mean Leighton was the one who for sure did. Bellwether Tech is a large company with many employees. Then there's the people who don't work there who might be holding a grudge or fear that place."

"Then what about Leighton's call to me?" Aiden postured. "The timing of that can't be coincidental, right? That's too much."

"But just because he called doesn't mean he was here. Or that the email came from him. Or that him not being able to be reached is for sure connected." He shrugged a little. "Coincidences are rare, but that doesn't mean they don't happen. Who knows, Leighton might have called you on the way to a vacation or some out-of-pocket trip with no service. He could be on a cruise."

"All right, you're reaching now, Mr. Bodyguard," Aiden said.

Mack held his hands out, palms raised in a giving-up gesture.

"I'm just saying, Mr. Potted Plant, that Leighton Hughes might be somewhere out there with no idea that you're looking for him."

Aiden opened his mouth. Then he closed it. Then he opened it again. He narrowed his eyes and locked in on the Bluebird Breeze. Was there a possibility that Leighton really had no connection to what was going on? That Bryce's murder, Bellwether Tech and the men who had tried to take him were their own circle in a graph while Leighton was the other with no overlapping in between?

Maybe Aiden was putting the two together. Maybe he was still touchy about what had happened. Maybe he still blamed Leighton, in some part, for his complicity. Maybe he still blamed himself for keeping quiet, and who better to shift that blame onto than the man who was beside him as he rose within the company?

"Ugh. This is too frustrating." Aiden balled his fists and shook them. "I'm going to try to get in," he decided. "This house might not be the smoking gun that leads us to Leighton, but its reservation is until the end of next week. So there might be something inside that makes this all make way more sense."

"We've already looked at all entrances," Mack reminded him, falling in step behind him as he charged to the front porch.

"Well, that was before we knew that this place had a weird connection to the chaos that's been our last week. That makes me more motivated to be detail oriented. Now, help me look again or be the silent, broody and attractive wall of bodyguarding prestige I know you can be and keep me covered."

Aiden peered through the windows as best he could now that he had a better reason to do a good job at looking. Before he'd been hesitant. Mainly for the fact that he'd worried he would be caught. Now he wanted to do the catching.

Mack did his job of being his cover and quietly followed Aiden around the house again. It's why he was able to hear Aiden's cry of excitement the second they both realized they had overlooked something on their first walk-around search.

"It's not actually locked!"

The Realtor lock on the back door was around the handle, but looking closer Aiden realized the latch wasn't all the way closed. Which meant at the moment it was just a complicated-looking door hanger.

Aiden reached out and tested the door itself. The knob turned, no issues.

Mack's hand wrapped around Aiden's wrist.

"And that's my cue." He pulled Aiden away from the door gently. "Stay here."

"The best you'll get is me standing behind you." Aiden hurried. His adrenaline was surging again. Whatever was inside would give them an answer they didn't already have. Whether that was being able to call this a dead end or that was them finding a lead that blew their amateur investigation right out of the water.

"You need to stay here," Mack tried again.

Aiden waved off the concern.

"You're supposed to guard my body, not tell my body to lounge on someone's back porch while yours goes inside. Now, let's hurry. I'm getting anxious over here."

Mack gave him one of his best sighs and then gave in. He let go of Aiden's wrist but only after angling in front of him.

Then he opened the back door, and the two of them went inside.

Bluebird Breeze was indeed empty. No one yelled at them in surprise, nothing jumped out at them as dangerous and there were no blatant clues that yelled out, "here's your answers" sitting around.

At least on the first floor.

Mack led Aiden up the stairs onto a small landing. It fed to three doors. The first was to a bedroom that looked untouched. The second was to a bathroom that seemed equally untouched.

The third was to the largest bedroom.

At first it seemed as uninteresting as the rest of the house, but there was more than the standard rental home furniture set.

On top of the desk situated along the wall when you walked in was a laptop. It was open and plugged in. There was a screen saver running, a spinning whirl of different-colored strands.

Mack stopped Aiden before his excitement could fully set in.

"The roadwork was a trap," he whispered. "This feels the same."

Aiden would have agreed, but something was already pulling him toward the laptop. A sticker was next to the trackpad. It was of the stars and moon.

Aiden knew it had cost almost ten dollars despite its small size.

He knew that because he'd been the one to buy it.

"You were wrong," Aiden said, stopping in front of the laptop, eyes still on the sticker. He felt Mack stop at his elbow.

"About what?"

Aiden woke up the machine by clicking the space bar.

The screen saver was replaced by the desktop. The background was a picture of two people enjoying a snowy landscape together, both bundled up and happily holding hands.

"This is Leighton's personal laptop," Aiden said, though he doubted he needed to explain that now. Standing next to Leighton in the picture was none other than Aiden.

"I guess he's connected after all."

Chapter Sixteen

The stars above him swirled electric blue and green. Mack watched as the LEDs scattered, faded and danced across the ceiling of the small room on a loop. The night was clear and probably had a much better view of actual stars, but Mack had been charmed by the fake ones inside Aiden's bedroom.

They made him feel like a little kid at an observatory. Sure, it wasn't the real thing, but there was a comforting magic to the show. It wasn't real, but that didn't mean it wasn't special.

Though he did suppress a chuckle when Aiden turned the night-light machine on without a second thought. Just as he had turned on the sound machine, handed Mack a vibrant floral quilt his grandmother had made him and put the llama-shaped pillow at the head of Mack's makeshift pallet on the floor.

These things were obviously part of Aiden's normal routine and, even though it was nowhere near what Mack was used to, Mack found some comfort in being included in it.

That comfort was an isolated event that didn't last as long as he would have liked. Less than an hour after the overhead lights had been switched off, Aiden let Mack know that sleeping wasn't going to happen for him.

"Are you awake?" he whispered, loud enough to hear

over the sound machine but soft enough that if Mack had been asleep he wouldn't have woken him. It was the most Aiden could have done to restrain himself if he had something on his mind. Which Mack had no doubt he did.

"Yeah. What's up?"

Mack was on the floor next to the bed and couldn't see Aiden from his point of view. Only the window and bedroom door. Still, he pictured Aiden rolling onto his side, a crinkle between his eyes, as he talked in his direction.

"I just can't get over a lot of things that happened this afternoon," he said. "I mean, it was too easy, right?"

Mack wasn't sure what Aiden had done to the laptop at Bluebird Breeze could be considered easy. Like he had done in the back seat of the truck, Aiden had used his computer skills to do several things Mack didn't understand. Instead of waiting until he was finished, though, Mack had insisted on a play-by-play.

That's how he had gotten a real-time rundown on Aiden's disbelief and pain.

"I just don't buy it," Aiden added on now. "Leighton is the bad guy? I mean, yeah, he wasn't the best boyfriend and he might have let a job confuse his principles, but a murderer?"

This wasn't a new train of thought from Aiden. He had said as much when they had first read the private messages between Leighton and Bryce Anderson. Messages that damned Leighton unconditionally.

"You read what he said yourself," Mack had to remind him. Though he made sure to keep his voice on the gentler side. "It was two pages of the two of them fighting about hiding the truth. Then Leighton told Bryce to meet him at the park. The same park he was killed at. Then Leighton went missing after that."

Aiden's face appeared over the side of the bed. His brow was indeed creased.

"But why? What was his motive?"

Mack propped his head up on the back of his arms.

"Bryce must have found out about the blackmail at Bellwether. Maybe instead of leaving like you did, Bryce wanted to make it public."

Aiden's face twisted. The shadows made his expression look even more severe.

"So Bryce was being a hero and, instead of me helping, I left opportunity for my ex to be the villain."

Aiden said it in his usual sarcastic way, but Mack knew there was hurt there.

"Your choice to trust Leighton doesn't mean any of this is your fault. In fact, if you had tried to go public first, who's to say you wouldn't have ended up with two bullets to the gut?"

Mack had meant to be comforting. Aiden disappeared from view with a loud, long sigh.

"I still can't believe Leighton did this," he tried again. "Not only did he have the conversation saved on a laptop, which he left at a rental, by the way, but his laptop was also left unlocked. No password. No PIN. Nothing."

Aiden's head appeared over the edge of the bed again.

"I know I've always been a lot more conscious of cyber-security than most since I kind of have a knack for hacking, but there's no way Leighton left his personal laptop that unprotected. It makes no logical, professional or tactical sense."

Mack couldn't argue with that. The best he could do

was offer a possible reason why the error in judgment had been made.

"In stressful situations, some people don't make the best decisions. Maybe he was rushing."

"Rushing to what?" Aiden hurriedly tacked on. "There was nothing else in that cabin. Just his laptop. Did he run in, plug it in, steal the Wi-Fi, then leave to…"

The shadows of his hands waved through the air. He wanted Mack to fill in the blanks.

Mack already had a theory for that.

"He could have been busy trying to get you." Mack's dislike of Leighton Hughes had tripled in size in the last six hours. The more he thought about him, the larger it would grow.

"You really think that's why he called me? He wanted to lure me somewhere?"

"It would make sense."

"Then why not answer when I called him back? Did he decide to change tactics to stay off the grid? But, if he did that, then why send the email? He had to have known I'd track the location and show up at the rental house. If that's what he wanted me to do, then why include Jonathan Smith in the plan?"

Aiden was talking fast again. Barely a breath in between questions.

"Maybe he got impatient. You did go to a party before finding the location of the email."

Aiden didn't immediately respond. After a few moments, Mack almost sat up to check on the man, but then the sheets rustled and the sound of him shifting preceded to Aiden getting off the bed. He had his pillow under one arm and his blanket under the other.

Mack started to sit up, confused, but Aiden didn't react to it. Instead he threw his pillow down on the floor. He lay down right next to Mack.

"But hear me out," Aiden started, not at all addressing his change in location. "The only connection we have between Leighton and Jonathan Smith is that Leighton's laptop was found in the rental that Jonathan's sister reserved. That in itself seems way too complicated to make sense if they are indeed connected. Who made the reservation? And why? If Leighton wanted to kill Bryce, isn't that too many unnecessary hoops to jump through? And, a better question, why the heck didn't Leighton kill Bryce in Nashville? Why travel to a small town where the body would immediately be noticed? How in the double heck does *any* of this make sense?"

Mack was still sitting up.

He only had one question currently.

"Why—why are you on the floor?"

Aiden didn't skip a beat.

"I was getting tired of talking to you without seeing you, and I doubted you'd take my offer to come up and stay on the bed," he explained. "Even though it's a king-size beast that takes up more than half of this dang room. When you said you'd be next to me until Leighton or those guys were found, I believed you. When you insisted on lying on this hard floor with only some sheets and a quilt, I thought you might be bluffing."

Mack didn't know what to do for a moment. They were simply talking about current events. Right? He cleared his throat and leaned back onto his pillow. There wasn't a lot of floor space before two grown men were sharing the area. Now Mack could feel Aiden's side dangerously close to his.

"Usually my clients aren't as relaxed as you," Mack said, shifting a little to create some more room. "They're not this talkative, either."

Aiden snorted.

"Don't act like you don't enjoy me. I'm a delight."

Mack took back his own trademark snort.

"You're confident. I'll give you that."

The stars overhead started their loop over. Two grown men lying under a child's night-light. How had his week home turned into this?

"What are you going to do now?" Mack laced his hands over his chest. The stars disappeared from his mind and were replaced by thoughts of the next week.

After finding the conversations between Leighton and Bryce on the laptop, Mack had called the sheriff's department. He had been hoping to get a different detective but knew that Winters would be the lead.

And he had been.

Though he'd been uncharacteristically quiet, the detective had said that they would get to the bottom of everything. Mack had expected suspicion, a scolding, too. Instead Winters had asked very little and said that he would be in touch.

His uncle had been the same way. When a case became too complicated, it was easier to let it go than dig in and hold on.

It's why no Atwood child could stand a Winters.

"I feel like I'm being forced into a waiting game," Aiden finally answered. "The only way to win at one of those is to do the one thing you can—wait. But that thought makes my skin crawl."

Mack could feel the breath Aiden let out.

"If Leighton is the big bad wolf and he killed Bryce, I'd like to find out exactly what Bryce knew."

"You think that it might not be Bellwether Tech related?"

Aiden didn't say anything for a bit. Mack turned his head to check on the man. His eyes were closed. He kept them that way when he answered.

"I think that Bellwether Tech might have more than the one skeleton in the closet. And maybe it's finally time that I do something about it."

Mack waited for a follow-up explanation. He didn't get one. The quiet sneaked back into the room and filled the spaces in between. Mack stayed just where he was as he watched Aiden lie still. It wasn't until sometime later that he realized the man had fallen asleep.

And, some time after that, Mack did, too.

AIDEN WOKE UP on the bed the next morning and had the time of his life trying to remember how he got there. He rubbed the sleep from his eyes, scoured every inch with his gaze after that, tried to recall the last thing he remembered and still came up with nothing.

One second he had been talking with Mack on the floor, and the next it was morning and he was snuggled up on his llama pillow.

"I didn't even drink," he breathed out to himself. He must have been more tired than he had realized to pass out that soundly.

Aiden peered over the side of the bed. His grandmother's quilt was folded neatly against the wall. Mack was nowhere to be found.

The smell of something delicious, however, was.

Aiden grabbed his cell phone off the charger and followed the scent down the hall.

What a sight he was met with.

Mack was wearing a dark blue tee, black pants and the llama-print apron Aiden had been gifted on his last birthday. He was standing at the stove, two skillets going at once. There was bacon in one and eggs in the other.

Aiden was immediately suspicious.

"Since when did I have food?"

Mack's professional bodyguard skills must have already been working. He didn't turn in surprise at Aiden's sudden appearance. Instead he shook his head.

"Unless you count junk food, you definitely didn't," he answered. "Lucky for us that Goldie was coming to town. She dropped these, and those, off."

He pointed around his arm to a box on the eat-in kitchen table.

"They're doughnuts from Sue and Mae's. She didn't know which you might like, so she got a spread."

Aiden's mouth was watering right alongside his chest filling with some warmth.

"No wonder you Atwoods are so popular in town. You're good hosts even when you're in other people's homes."

Mack grabbed a fork and went to flip a piece of bacon.

"Don't lump me in with the twins. This is the first time I've even cooked for someone other than them."

Aiden was glad that the bodyguard wasn't facing him. His face heated as if he was the one slaving over the stove.

Mack Atwood was cooking for him.

That was an achievement he had unlocked without realizing it was one he had wanted.

"Go wash up, and it should be ready when you're done," Mack added.

Domestic Mack Atwood.

It wasn't a bad look, that was for sure.

"Yes, sir."

Aiden washed his face, brushed his teeth and exchanged his pajama pants for joggers. He combed his hair, decided it needed some gel and went back to the bathroom to style it. Mack had gone through the trouble to cook; Aiden should at least go through the trouble of looking his best.

He nodded to himself, thinking that was a normal response to someone cooking for him, when his cell phone started vibrating in his pocket.

The caller ID stopped him in his tracks.

That's when he remembered something he didn't even realize he had forgotten.

He answered on the second ring.

"You thought I'd forgotten about you, didn't you?"

Jenna Thompson was as chipper as ever. In fact, the only thing that Aiden believed had changed about the woman since he had last seen her at Bellwether was her location. Instead of being in Nashville, she was settling onto the couch in Aiden's living room.

Aiden had been surprised by her call. Mack had gone quiet. He pulled a chair to a spot across the couch for Aiden to sit in. Then he stood next to it. He no longer had his apron on, but there was a spatula in his hand. If Aiden hadn't been so thrown by Jenna's call and then appearance, he would have teased the man.

Instead his focus zoomed in on the younger woman, who was all smiles.

"It was me who forgot," Aiden admitted. "So much has happened that my mind let it slip that I'd called you last week."

It was true. On both counts. Over the phone Jenna had told him she would call him back once she asked around about Leighton. She hadn't.

"But, even if you'd forgotten, you didn't have to come all this way," Aiden tacked on. "Another call would have been just fine."

At this Jenna's smile faltered. She glanced over at Mack, then back to Aiden.

"Oh, yeah, I'm sorry," he said. He held his hand out toward Jenna and did a late introduction. "Mack, this is Jenna Thompson. We worked together at Bellwether Tech. She's the lead assistant in the IT department. Basically one of the low-key superheroes of the department. I called her last week to see if she knew where Leighton was, since she usually knows everything there is to know in the department."

"It's the business," she commented.

"A business that I don't think many people would have done as well as you in."

Jenna waved through the compliment. Mack was still silent. His eyes were fastened to Jenna. Aiden continued the introduction.

"And Jenna, this is Mack Atwood. He's my—"

Aiden stopped middeclaration.

While he and Mack had used the term *bodyguard* several times, the fact of the matter was, Mack wasn't a true hired hand. They had no documents between them, no signatures or payments. Nothing other than verbal agreements that, if Aiden was being honest, he wasn't sure were completely sincere. It was something he had already thought about the night before when he couldn't fall asleep.

Mack was his bodyguard until they actually got down to the details. And if Mack didn't feel the obligation to be one? Would he leave? Would he end their partnership and head back into his quiet world at the Atwood estate before jetting off to a new job somewhere else?

Aiden didn't think Mack would simply abandon him, yet he hadn't been able to stop the wayward worry that it might happen if they really got down to what being his bodyguard really meant.

So, using the title out loud now to Jenna had him at a crossroad of crisis.

One that the man at the center of his worries pulled him out of with an absolutely bombshell of a redirect.

"I'm his boyfriend."

Chapter Seventeen

The words came out before Mack had realized he was going
to say them. Once they were out there, though, Mack didn't
take them back.

Aiden also didn't try to undo them.

Though Mack knew the man had been caught off guard.
His cheeks were a dark shade of red. Even his ears were
turning.

Jenna looked between them.

"Your boyfriend?" Her voice had gone a little flat.

Mack didn't like that.

He didn't like her, and he wasn't exactly sure why.

Maybe it had to do with the fact that she was from Bellwether and, like Aiden had said, instead of just calling she
had shown up at his home in Willow Creek.

Regardless of the reason, Mack had wanted a different
claim to Aiden. A way to show the woman that he was invested in Aiden. That he was on his side and not going
anywhere.

Thankfully, Aiden played along despite him being flus-
tered.

"He's my boyfriend," he repeated.

"You actually caught us about to have breakfast." Mack
placed his hand on Aiden's shoulder. His thumb was rest-

ing on the back. Mack put a little pressure into it. He hoped Aiden understood that he wanted the woman to explain why she was there sooner rather than later.

Aiden must have gotten the hint. He placed his hand over Mack's and patted it once.

"What can we do you for, Jenna? Did you really come all the way to Willow Creek to see me?"

Jenna's resting smile went flat, too. She sighed.

"Actually, I came because of our CEO. Not because of you."

Mack felt Aiden tense beneath his hand.

"What?"

Jenna pulled a card out of the purse on her lap. She handed it to Aiden.

"He was contacted by this detective from the sheriff's department here about Bryce's homicide investigation. He's there right now with his wife. I came down separately with Leighton's work laptop, as they instructed. Once I dropped that off, I realized I had been rude and never gotten back to you, so I thought I'd reach out."

Mack spied the business card over Aiden's shoulder. It belonged to Detective Winters. So he was actually investigating.

"I was also asked about Leighton's latest work activities," she continued. "I don't think I was much help, though. Other than to apologize for not getting back to you faster, I wanted to tell you in person that I have no idea where Leighton is or what's going on. I wanted to be helpful. I'm sorry." She glanced once again at Mack. He didn't know the woman but could tell she wanted some privacy from him.

Tough cookies.

Mack wasn't going to leave.

"Mack, could you go grab Jenna here a cup of coffee?" Aiden patted his hand again. "Please?"

He wanted privacy because he knew that's what Jenna wanted.

Mack held in his grumble.

If they had been in a public place, he wouldn't have moved from his spot, but since the kitchen was only a few feet away, he relented.

"Sure thing." He didn't bother to hide the tightness in his tone. Jenna, at least, seemed to be grateful. She was smiling again when Mack excused himself.

As soon as Mack was in the kitchen, he heard Jenna start up. Whatever she wanted to say, she had a lot of that something. She also kept that something on the quiet side. Mack could hear her talking but not the words themselves. It frustrated him. He was unkind to the coffee maker as he smashed the On button.

Why were so many Bellwether Tech people showing up in Willow Creek? He understood the investigation, but there seemed to be too many key players from Aiden's past moving around them.

If Detective Winters had called in the CEO and his wife, did that mean he had found out about the Bellwether blackmail?

The coffee started to brew. Mack used the sound to cover his backpedaling to the kitchen doorway. From his vantage point, he could only see Aiden's face. That was enough for him to know that whatever Jenna was saying had captured 110 percent of his attention. He had that crinkle between his eyebrows and was leaning forward slightly.

Mack wondered how much Jenna knew. If she was the head assistant of the IT department, didn't that mean she would have dealt directly with Leighton, Bryce and Aiden when everything had happened with the blackmail? Could she really not have known?

He backtracked to his phone on the table. He wasn't some pro hacker, but he could google Jenna's name to see if anything popped up. So far he had only seen the group picture with Aiden and Bryce after they won a bid. Everything else about Bellwether Tech had been text articles. He was good with faces, but names had never been his forte. If Jenna's name had been in an article, Mack might have missed it.

The sound of the coffee dripping continued as Mack brought up his phone's search engine. It filled the cup and stopped by the time he hit Enter on "Jenna Thompson, Bellwether Technologies."

The smell of the freshly brewed drink filled his nose as he clicked on the first article in the results.

It was about the newly appointed head of the IT department before Aiden's time. Her name was among the list of other hires, Leighton and Bryce included. There were two pictures. The first at the top of the story was of the department sitting around at their cubicles. Mack recognized Leighton at one desk, Bryce, too, farther away from the camera. The second picture was buried in the middle of the article.

It was of an older man in a suit posing with the group.

It was a man he recognized.

Every sense Mack had stopped. Every thought evaporated into the blank nothingness that had exploded around him.

He couldn't see or speak or hear or smell or figure out if his thoughts had stopped or were just going so fast he couldn't see them.

It was how Aiden was able to get in front of him without alerting Mack at all.

"Mack? Are you okay?" His voice broke through the nothingness as he took Mack's face in his hands. "What's wrong?"

Mack looked down into Aiden's eyes.

The forest.

All at once his thoughts shifted.

"You've never said the CEO's name. I've never seen his picture."

Aiden's eyebrow rose. He dropped his hands.

"I guess I haven't, but why does that matter?"

Mack held up his phone and pointed to the picture.

"Because I've seen him before. He was younger, but it's definitely him."

"Who?"

Mack didn't have to look again. He was, after all, a man with his own superpower. Someone who, once he saw a face, remembered it forever. The man had aged, but he was the same.

"This is the man who I'm sure killed my dad."

"What?" Aiden's gaze dropped to the picture while his pitch went sky-high in disbelief. "This is the man you saw running away from the fire? The client your dad reported? How is that possible?"

Mack was about to ask how Aiden knew about the warehouse fire, but Jenna walked into the kitchen, face blank.

"You're Malcolm Atwood?"

He couldn't read her expression. Aiden took his hand.

"Do you know him?" he asked.

She didn't answer right away.

She didn't get a chance to do it at all.

Someone knocked on the front door.

All three of them turned to face it.

The knock came again.

Mack addressed Jenna first.

"Was anyone else supposed to come here with you?"

She shook her head, but she didn't say no. Her eyes narrowed on the door as another knock sounded. Aiden squeezed Mack's hand.

"It could be the twins? Or Ray?"

"They would have warned me. Stay—"

Someone was unlocking the front door. Aiden shared a look with Mack. It clearly said that no one should have had a key to his home.

Mack was in the hallway in a flash. The sunlight that streamed in through the open door met the hardwood in front of him. It took him too long to realize what he was seeing.

Who he was seeing.

"You," he breathed out.

Leighton didn't take his time.

He pulled his gun up and shot.

AIDEN WAS GLAD THAT, for once, he was slow. While Mack, and even Jenna, had hurried into the hallway from the kitchen, Aiden had lagged. Like he had bad internet, his actions had taken a few beats too long. His software was processing too much, and his hardware couldn't keep up.

That's why he had one foot in the hallway and one in the kitchen when Leighton raised his arm.

Whatever lag Aiden had just experienced resolved itself. His hands wrapped around Mack's arm, and he pulled him backward with everything he had.

It might have been enough.

Mack yelled out just as Jenna screamed. Aiden didn't

know where she went, but he and Mack stumbled back into
the kitchen, nearly falling to the tile in the process. Mack
was quicker than that, though. He spun with their momentum, keeping them both on their feet while also pushing
them back farther into the room.

He shook Aiden off him and was going right back to the
hallway in one fluid motion.

"Mack!" Aiden yelled, but he had other things to do.

Leighton appeared in the doorway and crashed into the
wall that was Mack Atwood.

Another shot sounded. Aiden shouted as one of the cabinets along the wall seemed to explode. He couldn't help
but close his eyes and shrink in response.

When he opened them again, he saw Mack connect a fist
against Leighton's side. The other man bowed at the power.

He didn't drop the gun.

Mack had one hand around his wrist, struggling to get
control.

Then Jenna threw a lamp.

It was cheap and had been sitting on every living room
side table Aiden had ever had, but it was made of glass
and, apparently if thrown hard enough, it was mighty all
its own. It hit Leighton's shoulder and shattered. The impact and aftermath threw off the tussling men's balances.
Leighton went one way and Mack the other.

Jenna had wanted to help, but she had made an opening that only hurt.

Leighton hit the hallway wall; Mack hit the kitchen floor.

There was only a few feet of space between them, but
Aiden knew the problem as soon as the others did, too.

Mack wouldn't be able to get to Leighton or cover before
Leighton had the time to pull the trigger again.

That's when Aiden made a split-second decision.

He couldn't stop Leighton, but he could move enough to make a difference for Mack.

So, he did.

Every muscle in Aiden's body seemed to come alive. One second he was standing off to the side, terrified. In the next he was standing in front of Leighton and his gun, arms wide and sorry to no end that the last thing he would see wouldn't be the man on the floor behind him.

"No!" he heard Mack yell.

But it was too late.

The gunshot was so loud Aiden was sure the entire world could hear it.

His eyes closed on reflex. He braced for pain.

It didn't come.

At least it wasn't his.

Aiden opened his eyes. Leighton crumpled to the ground. The gun in his hand hit the floor and skidded in front of the refrigerator to their right.

Aiden didn't understand.

Why was Leighton on the ground? Why was there blood pooling from his side? Why wasn't it Aiden?

Two large hands wrapped around Aiden's arms. They spun him around.

It was Mack.

He was saying something, but Aiden couldn't make it out.

There was blood on Mack's arm.

"Are you hurt?" Aiden heard the absolute panic in his question. Mack seemed to be taken aback by it, too. His eyes widened.

"I'm fine," Mack said. "Are you? Aiden. Are you?"

Aiden nodded.

It must have been enough for the bodyguard. His expression softened.

"I want you to stand right here. Don't turn around, okay?"

Aiden nodded again.

"Jenna? Keep the gun on him for a second, okay?" Jenna yelled from the other room that she understood.

Was she the one who had shot Leighton? Aiden had a lot of questions. Instead of asking any of them, he decided to listen to Mack.

He stood still and he didn't turn around.

Chapter Eighteen

The deputies from the sheriff's department didn't arrive until half an hour after three people had been shot inside Aiden's home. The ambulance was slow, too. The twins were faster. Goldie screeched up in her small four-door first. She took Jenna and was off to Harper Faith like the mama she was. Finn came in right after. He had to slow down, because Leighton had needed all the help he could get, even while being moved to the truck.

Finn wasn't a doctor, but working in the medical field had taught him a thing or two, so he became their make-shift EMT in the back of Mack's truck. Aiden became his assistant, as much as Mack wished he didn't have to deal with any of it. They had run out of options, though. Mack refused to let Leighton die in Aiden's home. The memory of the fight alone was bad enough.

But Mack needed to drive like the true local he was and get everyone to the hospital as quickly and safely as possible, so Aiden sat in the back seat doing the best he could with triage using a roll of paper towels. Because, as he later told Mack in a quiet voice, he'd been worried about staining Mack's truck.

They all made it in good time. Ray had lit the beacon ahead of them, and ER nurses and staff had been waiting for their arrival. Leighton had gone to surgery, Jenna had been taken to a room and when Mack was getting his graze cleaned in one of the emergency room cubes, he found out why the response to his call had been so slow.

"Caleb Holloway and his wife were run off the road over on the Danberry Bridge," Ray explained.

Caleb Holloway. The CEO of Bellwether Tech. The man Mack had seen running away from the warehouse fire, despite no one believing him.

"Both were sent to Nashville in critical condition," he continued. "I think the wife is being airlifted somewhere else up north."

His face was drawn. Severe. Mack didn't understand why. Only Aiden and Jenna had heard his realization about the connection between the CEO and his father's death. He hadn't had time to tell anyone else yet.

"Who ran them off the road?" Mack asked. "Was it Leighton?"

Ray shook his head.

"Whoever did it wrecked the truck and took off before anyone could respond." His expression only soured further. "Mack. It was your truck. The one that you were driving when those guys stopped you and Aiden."

They let that sit for a few moments.

"I guess Detective Winters and I are going to have a lot to talk about when he gets here," he said.

Aiden came back with Finn then. They had gone to his office for some extra work shirts. Both had been covered in blood. None of it theirs. There were still some on their pants, but it would have to sit for a while. No sooner had they walked into the cube did deputies start coming in. Detective Winters wasn't far behind.

"I'll take you to Aiden's house," Mack had told the detective. When the man didn't like the directive, Mack made sure his bottom line was clear. "Aiden stays here with Marigold and Finn."

The detective must have been really stressed. He had thrown his hands up and said he didn't care. If Mack had been on better terms with him, he would have felt some sympathy. Instead the detective followed him to Aiden's, where Mack walked him through everything that had happened.

"Jenna had a small handgun in her purse. After she threw the lamp, she pulled it out and shot. I was able to grab Leighton's gun after that." Mack felt rage course through him. His hand fisted at his side. It took effort to unclench his jaw to speak again. "If it wasn't for her, this would have been a lot worse."

The detective rubbed the back of his neck.

"Looks to me like if the assistant of the year wasn't packing, Mr. Riggs sure wouldn't be walking around. I guess he decided to play bodyguard, huh?"

Mack had to double down on his effort to keep his rage from coming out.

The detective pulled his phone out and read a text.

He cussed low.

"This entire thing is a whole cluster, and I'm not even sure where that cluster starts." He opened another text. Mack could see the sheriff's contact name as the sender. "But I can only do so many things at once."

He looked down at the blood on the floor. He sighed.

"Come to the department tomorrow. Bring Bodyguard Riggs. I'll keep tabs on Ms. Thompson and Leighton Hughes. I can't help thinking that half of our problems are because your group keeps nosing into problems that aren't yours. Go home tonight and stay there. Don't give us any more headaches. Okay?"

Mack decided then to sit on the fact that Caleb Holloway was the same man Detective Winters's uncle had insisted was innocent all those years ago.

"We'll try our best to avoid all the bad guys you're having trouble catching," Mack snapped back. "Just try to do a better job, okay?"

Detective Winters looked like he was sizing Mack up.

Then he must have decided against doing anything more.

He left Aiden's house and took the last of the deputies with him.

Mack looked back at the blood on the hardwood.

That could have been Aiden's.

It was Mack's turn to cuss. He didn't do it low.

After that things became calm in comparison. Jenna, who had taken the first shot to her arm, was resting. Ray said he would keep an eye on her during his night shift and told the Atwood siblings and Aiden in no uncertain terms to go home. Mack was more inclined to listen to him over Detective Winters. The four made their way to the Atwood home as the sun set. Finn made sure they ate some food, Goldie prepared the guest bedroom and when Aiden insisted he didn't want to be a burden by staying, the twins refused to let him leave.

"We know what you did for us," Goldie said. Her eyes cut over to Mack. "You didn't have to be his shield, but you still did it. Even if it didn't come to that, you put yourself in harm's way to protect one of us. Which makes you one of us. So, you're staying here tonight. Finn will have some clothes that should fit you, and we have extra toothbrushes in the guest bathroom. Anything else, you ask."

Mack had waited for Aiden to fight that again, but he relented with a quiet thank-you. The twins excused themselves to their rooms. Mack was supposed to guide Aiden to the guest bedroom, but he didn't. Instead he took him right to his room.

He shut the door behind them.

It was the first time they had been alone since that morning.

Mack was having a hard time speaking.

So, he didn't.

He closed the space between himself and Aiden in less than two steps. He closed the space between their lips even faster.

Mack hadn't meant for the kiss to be as hard as it was, but there was no denying its force. All the anger at Leighton, at himself, at Aiden for uselessly putting himself in danger came out. It pushed his lips against Aiden's with a sense of relief pulsing through.

He was angry that Aiden could have been hurt, or worse, because of him.

He was angry that Aiden had gone through so much in the last week.

He was angry that he hadn't done more for him. That he hadn't said more.

But Aiden was okay. He was here. Mack could see him, could feel him.

He softened the kiss and then broke it.

If Aiden reciprocated, he didn't know.

Mack was just glad he was there.

He rested his forehead against Aiden's and spoke in a whisper.

"My favorite color is green, my first job was a cashier

at the dollar store and my childhood best friend's name is Raymond Dearborn."

Mack felt Aiden's brow crinkle beneath him.

"Huh?"

Mack took a moment before he stepped back from the man.

"Yesterday you said you could destroy me if you knew those things about me," he explained. "I'm here to tell you that you have my full permission to do that. You, Aiden Riggs, can destroy me but, please, promise me that you will never, ever do that again."

When Aiden didn't respond, Mack took his chin in his hand.

"Promise me," Mack repeated. "Please."

Aiden's voice was soft, but Mack still felt it in his chest. "I promise."

THE SHOWER HAD no chance of waking Aiden up. Simply for the fact that Mack had already done a thorough job of it.

Aiden was wrapped in a towel and staring at the mirror. It was partially fogged up, but he could still see how overwhelmed he was written right there in his reflection. So much had happened within the span of a few hours. So much that he had begun to feel numb somewhere between rushing Leighton into the hospital to watching Mack leave the hospital with Detective Winters.

Aiden had just stopped feeling.

Whether it was because everything was too much or a defense mechanism, he wasn't sure. He had simply decided to go with the flow with as little resistance as possible. He figured maybe that way he could make it to the end of whatever was going on.

Then Mack had kissed him.

It was like their roles had reversed. Aiden felt Mack's emotion, heard it, too, and watched as the quiet man of muscle and brawn had sunk a bit. He hadn't commanded Aiden to stay safe. He had been begging. And Aiden had barely reacted. He had agreed, sure, but when Mack stepped away from him and directed him to the bathroom, Aiden had simply gone.

He'd even taken the bag that Mack had packed for him at his house without a word.

That bag was resting on the counter. Aiden let his hand drop and opened it to see exactly what Mack had thought to take.

Only seconds rummaging inside it and Aiden knew two things without a doubt.

One, Mack hadn't just thrown the first thing he saw into the bag. He had taken his time and been thoughtful about it. He had listened to Aiden when he had been rambling about his favorite sleep clothes, he had made sure to get the right toiletries, including his hair gel, and even his box of accessories had made it inside, his favorite ring on top. Mack had also packed his favorite joggers and several carefully folded shirts that had been hanging in his closet. But, the item that really got Aiden was the one he had been most self-conscious about when Mack had first come into his room.

He had packed Aiden's night-light that projected stars.

Aiden ran his finger along the power cord. It was wrapped carefully around the base.

That's when Aiden came across the second thing he knew without any doubt.

He kept the realization to himself as he changed and went back to the bedroom.

Mack had a comforter and pillow in his arms. He nodded to the bed.

"You sleep here, and I'll take the floor. I already found a place to set up the stars, and the sound machine can go—"

"I want you to stay with me." The words came out strong. True. Aiden went to the bed. "Here, I mean. Not on the floor."

He slid under the covers and closed his eyes. His heartbeat was racing, but he felt oddly calm despite it.

Mack didn't respond. At least not in words. A few minutes passed before Aiden felt the bed dip down a little next to him. The sheets and comforter rustled as he settled beneath them. A soft click sounded. Aiden opened his eyes just as the stars from his projector scattered across the ceiling.

He watched them for a moment.

Then Aiden rolled over to face Mack.

He wanted to say a lot, to shower the man in thank-yous and I'm sorrys. Tell him that he liked him, that he was glad he'd met him and wanted to see him a lot in the future. He wanted to ask him about his feelings, not for him but for everything. He wanted to know his favorite song and his most exciting stories from his job. He wanted to ask where the baby pictures were, if his college experience had been fun and what the Atwood patriarch had been like.

Aiden wanted more of Mack, and he had every urge to start right then and there to get it.

But, when he rolled onto his side, Mack was already there staring across his pillow at him.

All questions and conversation ended right there before they ever started.

Aiden didn't want to talk anymore.

He placed his hand on Mack's chest. He placed his lips on his next.

Unlike the kiss earlier, this one was soft. Calm.

Aiden hoped it soothed Mack of every one of his troubles.

And Mack took the kiss like Aiden had earlier. He was still until Aiden pulled away.

For a moment, he worried that he had misunderstood. That Mack hadn't wanted to be this close.

That worry didn't last long.

Mack wrapped his arms around Aiden and pulled him closer. This kiss went deep. After that there was no more one-sided anything.

Aiden responded to his lips with a ferocity that he felt in every part of his body. His hands slid up Mack's chest and grabbed onto his shoulders. One went farther up and wound into his hair. It acted as an anchor as Mack deepened their kiss even more. His tongue parted Aiden's lips, and together they started to explore each other's mouths.

Mack tasted like peppermint.

Aiden wanted more.

Apparently so did Mack.

When Aiden started to pull up the edge of Mack's shirt, Mack broke their kiss long enough to throw it off himself. It disappeared into the darkness of the rest of the room. Aiden's disappeared next.

With a new area to explore, Mack did just that.

He took Aiden's wrists, pinned them and him against the bed and rolled over on top. Mack straddling him was a sight to see. It was, however, a feeling that Aiden didn't think he would ever forget.

He took the small space of time where their lips weren't touching to do his own exploration.

Aiden trailed his hands across Mack's bare chest.

No doubt, Michelangelo would have sold his soul to sculpt such a man.

Aiden was about to say so when he came to the bandage on his side. It was small but blaringly there.

Mack must have sensed the mood had paused. He looked down as Aiden lightly touched the spot next to it.

"It doesn't hurt," Mack said. His voice was soft, a whisper. Aiden wasn't sure he trusted it. If Mack was in pain, would he really admit it?

Mack lowered himself. The kiss he gave Aiden next was brief. He ran his hand along his jaw, his thumb trailing across Aiden's lips next. Mack's gaze stayed there as he spoke again.

"But, if it did, would you distract me if I asked you to?"

Aiden was already 100 percent in, but the smirk that grew along Mack's face sealed every deal there ever was or would be.

He nodded.

"I'll see what I can—"

Mack cut him off with another kiss that spoke to every inch of Aiden's body.

There was no more talking after that.

Chapter Nineteen

Mack woke up warm.

The man lying against his chest was only partially the reason. Sunlight was pouring through the window over the bed. He'd slept through the night. Soundly, too.

Aiden shifted against him. Mack readjusted the arm he had around him. Aiden tensed but didn't say anything for a few minutes. Finally, Mack chuckled.

"Let me know when you're done pretending to be asleep and I can tell you good morning," he said.

Aiden pulled the covers up to cover the bottom half of his face. He spoke against Mack's chest.

"I wasn't pretending to be asleep," he defended. "I thought you might be and didn't want to wake you. It's called being considerate."

Mack smiled and ruffled Aiden's hair. The contact only seemed to make his new anxiety worse. He did a little shimmy away from Mack's hand and tried to put distance between them.

Mack didn't allow it. He let Aiden put his head on the other pillow but kept his hold around him.

"No need to be shy now," Mack pointed out. "So why don't we lie here for a little longer before we get the Atwood twin interrogation that's surely waiting outside that door?"

Aiden met his gaze with wide eyes.

"What do you mean, the Atwood twin interrogation?" He lowered his voice but the panic was clear. "You don't think they know about us—about what we—" His cheeks turned a fun shade of red as he motioned between them.

Mack struggled to keep a straight face.

"I think the fact that you didn't sleep in the guest room might make them suspect that something happened," he stated, matter-of-fact. "But Goldie peeking in here an hour ago to check on us and seeing you in my arms might have been the real tip-off."

Mack couldn't help it. He smiled as Aiden's shade of red deepened. He pulled the covers up and over his head.

"Oh, my God." Aiden did another little shimmy in place. "How embarrassing. I'm so sorry."

He could feel Aiden try to pull away again, so Mack did his own pulling. He moved the covers and threw them down the bed. After their shower the night before, Aiden had changed into the sleep clothes Mack had packed, but now you would have thought with the way he scurried for the sheets that he was as naked as a jaybird.

"Why are you apologizing? It's not like you tricked me into this. I think it was me who actually started it."

Aiden slapped his hands on his face to hide.

"But I'm the one who told you to stay with me in bed."

Mack really couldn't help it this time. He let out a boom of laughter. Aiden peeked through his fingers at him.

"If you want to get technical, I'm the one who brought you to my room first."

Aiden didn't say anything. Mack sighed.

"If I regretted last night, I would have already left. Even if this was my room."

Aiden lowered his hands.

"What about the twins? Aren't they going to give you a hard time?"

Mack nodded.

"If you mean are they going to tease me like I did when Goldie and I found Finn making out with Lisa Perry in the living room to a 'sexy' music playlist, or when we caught *John* Perry, Lisa's cousin, sneaking out of Goldie's bedroom window wearing nothing but his boxers, then yes. They are going to give *me* a hard time. You? The second we leave this room, you'll probably be offered the best food we have."

Aiden didn't look too sure about that, but on cue his stomach growled.

That seemed to sway him. He lowered his hands. Mack felt him relax.

"I wouldn't mind eating anything at the moment. I only had a few bites of food yesterday."

Mack saw it then. He was pulling in all the memories of the day before. Worry pressed down on his expression. Mack wished he could fix it. The best he could do was make sure he was fed.

"Come on, then. Let's go get some food."

Aiden agreed, and any self-consciousness he had about the time they had spent together went to the back burner. He excused himself to the bathroom to get ready, and Mack threw on a shirt to go deal with the wolves first.

The wolves greeted him with twin grins in the kitchen.

Goldie did it over her coffee, Finn with a fresh pancake on his plate.

Mama Atwood spoke first.

"I know we don't often have people over, but maybe we can set up some kind of system where we lock our doors?

Or put a do not disturb *something* on the doorknob? Anything that would give us dear sweet siblings some privacy."

Mack rolled his eyes and pulled down two coffee cups from the cabinet.

"Or we could do this novel thing where we knock and don't just enter a bedroom unannounced."

Finn laughed.

"That's what I told her, but she insisted on checking on you since you never sleep in like that," he said. "I tried to stop her, honest."

Goldie swatted at her twin.

"You tried to stop me, my butt!" she exclaimed. "I'm the one who had to stop *you* from sneaking a peek once I told you those two were in bed."

Finn shrugged.

"Hey, you already ripped that Band-Aid off, so me looking didn't really do any more damage."

Mack got Aiden's cup of coffee brewing. He leaned against the counter as he waited.

"You two go ahead and get it all out," he said, crossing his arms over his chest. "Aiden's already worried."

Goldie looked like she was teeing up to explain there was no reason to be worried, but Finn had questions and knew he had to get them off quick.

"So what's up with you two? Are you guys together now? How long has this been going on? Who initiated it? Who was the big spoon? I feel like it would be you just because of the height difference, but also I've seen the way you look at Aiden when he isn't looking and I think you'd let yourself be a little spoon for him. Also, Goldie said there were stars in your room? What's up with that?"

For a second Mack was too stunned to respond. Goldie, however, nodded.

"I want all those answers, too," she said. "Also, how are your wounds? Did you hurt them? How do you want us to act when he comes in?"

Mack knew that, based on his personality, he should have been annoyed at the barrage of questions. That his introverted self should have felt the need to slough off any chance of him answering like he was in some kind of post-game media interview.

Instead, he felt pure love for his siblings.

Not a day went by when they didn't love and support him.

And not a day would go by when Mack didn't do the same for them.

So, he decided to answer them out of familial trust, loyalty and love.

However, that didn't mean he was giving them all the details.

Mack took a deep breath then rattled off the answers he was willing to give.

"We haven't talked about any of this at length. I kissed him first. It's not your business who was the big spoon or little spoon. Aiden sleeps with a star projector that's actually pretty nice. My chest and side wounds are healing fine, so there's no issue there. As for how to act, be yourselves." He narrowed his eyes at Finn. "But all intimate questions I ask you to keep to yourselves or I'll sock you upside the head. Got it?"

The twins used their powers to sync up.

They both saluted at the same time.

"Accepted terms."

"Yes, sir."

Aiden's coffee was ready. Mack turned to make himself a cup and smiled once his back was to his siblings.

He wasn't a fan of returning to Willow Creek, but he would never grow tired of being with Goldie and Finn. Along with Ray, they were his people.

By the time Mack's coffee finished, Aiden made his appearance in the kitchen. He had changed into the outfit Mack had packed, styled his hair and put on what Mack suspected was his favorite ring. He smiled sheepishly and said good morning.

Goldie was up in a flash.

"Good morning," she sang back. "Go ahead and sit down and I'll make you a plate. Do you like pancakes? If not we have some muffins I bought yesterday from the bakery. They're still absolutely delicious."

"Can confirm," Finn added. He held up a muffin wrapper. "I already demolished two of them as soon as I opened my eyes this morning."

Aiden said he was good with pancakes and settled opposite Mack's open seat at the table. Goldie made him a plate, Mack slid over the coffee and Finn pushed over the fruit plate he and Goldie had been snacking on. Aiden was a chorus of thank-yous, and when Mack sat down, he shared a quick look with him. His eyebrow seemed to raise in question. Mack smiled into his coffee.

And that was that.

The four of them ate their breakfast while enjoying small talk about nothing in particular. It was a skill to avoid all the things they could have been talking about. A skill that only extended until the dishes and food had been cleared away.

Mack wasn't happy to be the one to drag them back to the reality, but he didn't think he could put it off any longer.

He opened his mouth to start in when Aiden surprised him. His leg reached out under the table and pressed against the side of Mack's. It wasn't a playful touch. Somehow Mack knew it was Aiden's way of letting him know he wanted to speak first.

"Only a handful of people know what I'm about to say, but I think it's only right for you to know." He was talking to the twins. "I'm not exactly sure how it plays into what's been happening, but I've made a decision and it needs some context."

Mack pressed his leg against Aiden's beneath the table as he listened to him explain why he had left Bellwether Tech. It was the same story he had already told Mack, but this retelling was stone-cold. Facts, no emotion. Maybe that made it easier. Maybe that made it harder. Either way, the twins listened with rapt attention.

"I've thought about it since the hospital yesterday, and the best I can guess is Leighton was trying to cover for the CEO," he said once the story had been told. "I'm not sure how Bryce figured into it, but maybe he also found out like I did. I—I never thought Leighton was the kind of man who could…who could kill, but I'm guessing I was on his list."

The twins had taken the story in stride.

Goldie's eyebrows drew together in thought.

"So we think Leighton went after Holloway? That's why he and his wife were run off the road."

Aiden shrugged.

"Maybe Holloway realized that Leighton was trying to cover things up and only making matters worse and tried to turn him in? Or betray him? I don't know. That's one of many questions I wish I could ask Leighton right now."

"Have y'all told Winters yet? Or the sheriff?" Finn asked.

In unison Mack and Aiden shook their heads.

"I've decided I want to tell them today at the department," Aiden said. He looked to Mack. "I should have come clean about this before ever coming to Willow Creek but, well, I trusted the wrong person. Now I'm going stop putting it on other people and tell the truth myself. Holloway needs to be held accountable for what he's done, and if I can help, I'm going to do it, no matter what."

He gave Mack a significant look.

He had made an opening for him but hadn't forced the next issue.

Mack was thankful for it.

He took a deep breath in and let it out slowly.

"Which brings me to something I haven't had the chance to tell you two yet." Aiden pressed his leg back into Mack's. It was oddly reassuring. He dived in. "The client Dad reported to the sheriff's department after they attacked him. The guy I saw leaving the warehouse during the fire? I found out yesterday that he's Caleb Holloway. The CEO of Bellwether Tech."

This time the twins were a lot more vocal.

They, however, did not ask if he was sure.

"What?" they said together.

"But I thought he left Tennessee and never came back," Finn said.

"To be honest, I stopped looking into it when I started my career as a bodyguard." Mack glanced at Goldie, but he said the next part to Aiden since he was the only one who didn't know. "The boss who handles my contracts warned me that I was getting too obsessed with trying to figure out a way to prove that the fire wasn't an accident. I tried to find a way to connect it with the client, but I had a hard time finding anything. I might not have even remembered the name since I never imagined he would amount to anything like a CEO of a big tech company. His face, though—that I'll never forget."

Aiden nodded. He was crestfallen in the next second.

"I just hate that I've brought this to y'all," he said. "My ex-boyfriend hurt you, tried to do worse and then my ex-employer…did that to your dad." He let out a little laugh filled with sorrow. "If I had never come to Willow Creek—"

"Then no one would know Bellwether Tech needs to be taken down," Mack interrupted. "You didn't create these problems—you were just the unlucky one who realized they were there."

Finn agreed.

Goldie was hesitant, but not at that.

"Ray said that Caleb Holloway and his wife were taken to a hospital up north, a private one with a ton of specialists. It sounded like he might not make it."

They became silent at that.

Mack had thought about Holloway a lot the day before while cleaning Aiden's floors.

"Proving that he was at the warehouse the day of the fire, we know, is a hard ask, since all we have to go on is my memory. Proving after all these years that he started the fire? Probably impossible." Mack had also already made a decision. "As much as I hate it, I want us to only focus on what's happening now."

He counted each point out on his fingers.

"Aiden finds proof that the CEO used Bellwether Tech security footage to blackmail a user. Aiden loops in his boss, Leighton, and is told the situation has been handled. Aiden leaves when no harsher punishment is given and comes to Willow Creek. Over six months later, he gets a call from Leighton the morning after Bryce Anderson, who also worked at the company, is killed at the park, along with an anonymous email warning him about Bellwether Tech. Leighton goes missing, and Jonathan Smith attacks Aiden in his car." He took his five points and made a fist on the tabletop. He continued with the other hand.

"The next day, at least two men come to take Aiden, but instead all they get is my truck. Once me and Aiden are out of the hospital, we finally follow the address that the email was sent from to Bluebird Breeze, where we find Leighton's damning laptop. We loop in Detective Winters, and Leighton becomes suspect number one in Bryce's homicide case, which brings the Bellwether Tech top echelon to Willow Creek. The CEO and his wife are run off the road by someone in my missing truck, and Leighton comes to my house with a gun he definitely wasn't afraid to use." Mack had one finger left. He folded it and made another fist. "And that brings us to now."

They fell into another little silence. Aiden didn't look like he would be the one to break it. Finn did after a long drink of his coffee.

"If Holloway and his wife hadn't been run off of the road with your truck by those men, it would sound like Leighton was behind it all," he said. "But those men don't make sense in that scenario. Who are they and why did they seem to target the Holloways?"

"They could work for Leighton," Mack supplied. "Maybe something went sour between him and the CEO. Maybe the best way he thought to cover himself was to take out the only other person who knew about the blackmail."

"Assuming this is about blackmail at all." Aiden was quiet, but his words held an undeniable weight. He went on to explain without them needing to ask. "We think this is all about covering up the blackmail, but we haven't actually found any proof that it's connected. What if this isn't about the blackmail at all? What if we're focusing on the wrong thing?"

That stopped Mack.

Only because he was right.

Had they ever confirmed that any of this was connected to the blackmail?

Aiden followed up with a simple conclusion.

"We need to talk to Leighton," he said. "He's the only one who can give us answers at this point."

Mack didn't correct him, because he surely wasn't wrong. Aiden and those forest green eyes were all on him.

"Let's go to the hospital before we talk this all out with Detective Winters," he added. "I also want to check in on Jenna."

"We can bring her some food," Goldie suggested.

Finn nodded.

"Ray should be at the hospital finishing up, too," he said. "We should feed him, especially after what he did yesterday."

At the time, checking on Leighton's status, visiting Jenna and bringing some cheer to Ray after a long shift made sense.

So, Mack agreed to it.

That's how everyone Mack cared about ended up going to Harper Faith that morning.

And that's why, hours later, Mack would be fighting to save them all.

Chapter Twenty

Everyone split up.

Goldie took a bag of food to Ray's office in the basement of the hospital. Finn and Mack went to the postsurgery floor to get an update on Leighton's condition. Aiden went to the fourth floor of the main building to visit Jenna. He also had food for her but wasn't sure what she could and couldn't eat. She had been shot in the arm and had surgery, but everything had been a success.

Aiden knocked, worried he might disturb her, but found her sitting up with a magazine and smiling after he was told to come in.

Give it to Jenna Thompson—she was always chipper.

"Well, look who it is," she said in greeting. "What brings you here this early? Is everything okay?"

Aiden shook the bag in his hand.

"Food delivery and general inquiries about your health and happiness, madam."

Jenna took the food with a laugh.

"Well, isn't that the sweetest, sir." She placed it on the table positioned over her lap. Her phone vibrated, and she typed out a quick text, then motioned to one of the chairs next to the bed. "I thought after all the excitement yesterday you would still be in bed. At least, that's where I would be.

I just came in on the tail end of your adventure and can't believe all the things you guys have been through."

Aiden gave a pointed look at her bandaged arm. "I think you've been through more than I have," he said.

"Hey, now, that's a good thing. So don't you dare do that brow crinkle and feel bad. None of this is your fault. Okay?" Aiden smiled to be polite. The guilt in him didn't ease. He also wasn't sure what all Jenna knew. She made a show of looking back at the door. "Where's your boyfriend?"

Aiden felt some heat crawl up his neck a little. Waking up in Mack's arms had been a surprise, despite knowing that he had gone to sleep within them. The morning light had made what felt like a dream extremely real. And when things became real, they had a better chance of someone regretting them.

That's what Aiden had worried would happen with Mack. That he would wake up and regret everything. That the kiss had been impulsive and their night together was just two people thankful to be alive. But, even before Aiden had opened his eyes, he had known that for him there was no regret. That wanting to be close to Mack wasn't just because they had gone through danger and barely made it out alive.

Aiden cared about Mack. When the danger was there, when it wasn't, when they were with his family, when they were alone. Did Mack feel the same way or was he still just wrapped up in the mystery that had taken them all in?

Aiden wasn't sure.

But, for now, even the mention of Mack made him heat.

Jenna's eyebrow rose in question.

He had taken too long to answer.

He tried to play it off.

"Oh, uh, he's with his brother and sister in the basement." Aiden decided to lie simply because he didn't want to involve Jenna any more than she already was. She didn't need to know that Mack and Finn were seeing if they could talk with Leighton. Though he did realize his answer was confusing, too. "Ray—I mean, Dr. Dearborn—has an office there. They are all very close and brought him some food, too."

"Wow. Those Atwoods sure are nice. I get why people move to small towns if there are people like them around."

Aiden felt a flare of pride.

"They definitely make this place better, that's for sure."

Jenna was watching him intently. Aiden wondered if it was so obvious that his feelings were a lot more invested in the family than if they were just friends. He wanted to change the subject but wasn't sure the right way to go. So, he stuck with the theme of family.

"Are you expecting anyone from Nashville to come today? Or have you told anyone that you were hurt yet?" He imagined her on the phone telling her family and friends back home that she was A-okay and not to worry about her. That, like Mack, she had only gotten a flesh wound when in reality she had been shot.

Jenna laughed.

"Don't worry, my family knows I'm here." Her smile faltered. "They can't come right now, but I'm okay."

Aiden felt another flare of emotion. This one was sympathy.

"Well, I'm here if you need anything," he said. "After we go to the sheriff's department, I'll come back here and hang out with you, too. Tell me what you want for lunch, and I'll make it happen."

Her smile came back.

"Mack Atwood might be helpful, but I'll always be Team Riggs. You've always been so considerate."

Aiden snorted. He was about to make a joke about doing the bare minimum but, just like that, a memory resurfaced. With it, a question.

"By the way, how did you know about Mack before you met him?"

Jenna's brow creased. She tilted her head a little in question.

"What do you mean?"

Aiden didn't have to think on it too long. Even though a lot had happened after it, he still remembered her words verbatim.

"'*You're* Malcolm Atwood.' That's what you said in the kitchen before Leighton showed up," he said. "You seemed to have recognized him after he spoke about CEO Holloway."

A knock sounded on the door. Jenna's demeanor changed with it.

"Come in," she called. Her voice dipped lower. Aiden realized that she was wearing lipstick. It was red and neat.

A tall man with a buzz cut walked in. Jenna didn't say a greeting. She didn't say anything to him as he shut the door behind him.

Aiden looked expectantly at the woman to introduce them, but she remained quiet.

Her earlier smiles, all chipper and polite, twisted into a smirk. It felt like the Jenna before had gone and the Jenna that was there now had something to say.

"Since we're strolling down memory lane, I lied about something when I first came to your house," she said. "I might as well come clean now. Remember when I said I had forgotten about you?"

Aiden nodded on reflex.

The man at the door crossed his arms over his chest and leaned back against the door.

Aiden realized too late what was happening.

Jenna's smirk deepened.

"I never forgot about you, Aiden Riggs," she said. "I was just saving you for last."

LEIGHTON WASN'T AWAKE. His doctor didn't think he would be for a while. It was frustrating. Finn patted Mack on the back once they said their goodbyes to the doctor.

"We knew there was a good possibility that he wouldn't be able to talk when we came," Finn tried. "At least we know he's out of the woods."

Mack was grateful for that. As much as he didn't care for Leighton, he wanted his answers. Rather, he wanted Aiden to have those answers. It wouldn't make his pain go away, but it would help knowing the truth. At least, he hoped.

"I'm glad Aiden didn't come with us to see him, though," Finn added. "I know it's his ex and all—an ex who tried to kill him—but seeing him still has to be weird. They dated for a while and were friends afterward. No matter what happened, there's got to be some complicated feelings there."

"Why do you think I didn't fight Aiden on going to see Jenna instead?"

Finn put his arm around Mack's shoulder and swayed them both.

"Whoa, look here everyone. Mack got himself a boyfriend and is all in touch with other people's emotions. Love it. Love the energy. Keep up the good work, my dear sir."

Mack snorted and shook Finn off.

"Aiden isn't my boyfriend," he said. "I only said that to Jenna so she knew I was on his side no matter what."

"But you want him to be your boyfriend, right?" They had made their way to the main building's lobby. The central elevators had a few people waiting for them. Mack wanted to keep their private talk private, so he held his brother back to finish the conversation.

"I think there's been a lot going on for him," he said.

"You mean just because you were the spoons last night doesn't mean you're suddenly both in the same utensil drawer."

Mack rolled his eyes.

"You and this spoon thing. But, yeah, I guess. I think it might be too much for him."

"It's not the right time," Finn stated.

"It's not the right time," Mack repeated.

"You need to take him on a date first. Be romantic or else he might realize you aren't good boyfriend material. No. That's smart. I understand. Good move."

Mack had started walking again, thinking the conversation was at a close, but paused at that.

"What do you mean, I'm not good boyfriend material?"

Finn held his hands up in mock defense.

"Hey, I've never seen you in action. You might have inherited Goldie's awkwardness. Remember the last guy she was with? She tried to take him to that really weird art festival and ended up in a performance art play where they got paint thrown on them."

Mack held back his laugh out of respect for his sister. It was a hard feat.

"When I take Aiden on a date, I'll make sure not to accidentally stumble into an art exhibit," he deadpanned.

The elevators timed perfectly, both opening together. Mack watched two men get in one and another get into the second. The one with two men was headed down. The other was going up.

Finn started in that direction, no doubt wanting to catch a ride, but Mack stopped him once again.

This time, though, for a much different reason.

He recognized two of the men. One of them in the elevator going down had been wearing a worker's vest last time he had seen him. The one in the elevator going up was the man who had been in the car that had parked behind Mack's truck after the worker had stopped them.

The doors closed.

Everyone's here, Mack realized.

Out loud he turned to his brother and spoke quickly.

"Those are the men who came after us on the mountain. Two are going down to the basement. One is going up." Mack was already moving across the lobby to the door that led to the stairwell. The elevators at the hospital were notoriously slow. It was the only saving grace they might have at the moment. "Run ahead, and you, Goldie, and Ray get out of their way and call the cops."

Finn only had one question.

"What about you?"

"I'm going for Aiden."

That was that. No more questions or conversation. They split up the second they were through the stairwell door. Finn ran down; Mack thundered up. He knew Finn could get to the morgue before the men. Then it would be three smart adults who knew the hospital like the back of their hands. They could avoid the men until deputies came.

But Aiden and Jenna were sitting ducks.

And that was Mack's fault.

He took as many steps as he could, not breaking stride until he slammed into the fourth-floor exit. Mack still didn't stop as he turned left and ran to Jenna's hallway. Where he expected to be stopped by staff, he wasn't. He didn't have time to wonder why. Instead he didn't slow until he was at Jenna's door and throwing it open.

The room was empty.

"YOU KNOW WHAT everyone seems to overlook in hospitals?" Jenna spread her arms open wide. "The rooftops."

Over her shoulder was a view of treetops and a sliver of the town in the distance. Everything above was blue skies and sunshine. It would have been nice had Aiden not had a gun at his back since the stairs.

"No matter if you're in the city or a small, ridiculous town like Willow Creek, a hospital rooftop is just the best," Jenna continued. "Privacy with a breeze. You just can't beat that."

She was still smiling, but it was nothing like Aiden had seen before. There was an edge to it, a sharpness that wanted to cut.

Cut him, apparently.

"Why are we here, Jenna?" Aiden asked. "What do you want?"

She was wearing her hospital gown and her sling, but she was the picture of put together as she answered. It felt rehearsed, almost. Maybe it was. She tucked some of her loose hair behind her ear then nodded to the man behind him.

"Watch the door."

The man didn't hesitate.

That's when Aiden really felt it. Power.

Jenna Thompson was controlling things. What things, Aiden didn't know yet.

"What's going on?" he had to add.

Jenna took in a big breath of the fresh air. She looked at peace.

"This? This is about a little girl who decided it's better to be a knife in the back than a shield." She waved her hand at him, like a dismissal. "You don't understand, I get that. I didn't understand a lot in the beginning, either, but, don't worry, I'm here now to explain." She took a few steps toward him. The rooftop's ledge was several feet away. It made an already anxious Aiden even more so.

"See, I'm going to tell you a story, because I've always liked you, Aiden, and I want to give you a chance to make a good choice," she continued. "But, first, let's talk about the blackmail. You know, the one where our dear CEO Holloway found out that a user was having an affair and how he decided to use that against that poor, poor man." Her voice was dripping with sarcasm. "I wonder, did you ever see the actual video footage? I'm assuming you didn't."

Aiden shook his head.

"I was asked to loop footage. I didn't realize until later what it was for."

"Mmm. Sneaky." She sighed. "I figured you didn't see the actual footage or else you would have said something to me."

Aiden's eyebrow rose before he could force his facial expression to remain neutral.

Jenna didn't miss it.

"Everyone was so worried about the user that they never questioned his mistress. Who, by the way, was me." She held her hand out in a stop motion. "I know, I know. Plot twist, am I right? The executive assistant having an affair with a man right in front of her company's security cameras."

Aiden couldn't help it. He said the first thing that crossed his mind.

"It doesn't seem like the smartest move."

Jenna snapped her fingers.

"That would have been so careless of me, right? But what if I did it on purpose? What if I honey trapped the user to put him in a situation where blackmail was easy? What if, while making him fall for me, I got him front and center on his own personal home security system so the entire show was caught on camera? Would that make me less careless?"

Aiden's mind started racing.

"I would still call it a careless plan since Holloway found out."

"And what if I wanted that to happen, too? What if I knew he was keeping close tabs on me and left him a bread-crumb trail that led to my relationship as a mistress?"

She took another little step forward.

A breeze went by.

She kept going, seemingly enjoying herself.

"I know I may seem like the best company girl there is, but I actually hate two things very much." She held up her middle finger, winked and continued. "One, I absolutely despise the great and powerful Caleb Holloway. Despise him so much that I'd go around the world twice just to ruin his afternoon. Never mind his life." She held up her index finger. "Two, I think hate is a beautiful thing. Poetic. Classy. Love with nothing but consequence. Oh, and how I hate that man. So, I really hate it when the destruction of a person isn't a little dramatic. A little drawn out.

A little *unnecessary*. Why hate someone if you won't really punish them?"

Aiden didn't know if she wanted an answer and, if she did, he had no idea to which question she had posed. So when she paused, he asked his own.

"So you became a mistress to trap Holloway? But why would he care if you were a mistress? Why would he care about you at all?"

Her smile melted. The pristine posture she'd been holding herself with slumped a little.

"Oh, he doesn't care about me. Just the trouble I can make. I am his daughter, after all."

Aiden felt his eyes widen.

"What? You're his daughter? But—but he doesn't have any kids."

"Mmm. Believe me, how I wish that were true." She tapped her chest twice. "But me? I'm his only flesh and blood. I'm also his biggest embarrassment. See, my mother was in fact his mistress once upon a time. After she had me, she let him know and, well, that didn't go well. We were abandoned, forgotten. Left to poverty."

Her smile came back. It was razor-sharp.

"But then a miracle happened. When that great man got into some big trouble, he found me and used me as a shield. His poor, pitiful daughter *needed* her father. Nothing bad could happen to him if anyone could hear his equally pitiful story. So I was brought to his side and kept there until the trouble calmed down. A disposable pawn. A child with nothing, who would do anything for more. After that, though? I was sent back to that nothing. Back to the shadows. There I became a secret. How lovely, right?"

Aiden paused before speaking. Jenna let him.

"Are you—are you talking about the warehouse fire?" he asked. "That's how the man who was suspected of starting it got out of trouble. His daughter."

She tapped her chest again.

"You're fast," she said. "You'd think dear old Dad would have been more grateful for my amazing performance. Crying on the spot, yelling for him. Being pitiful and loud about it. Turning the weakhearted into the shameless who simply looked the other way. But, no. Instead that father of mine threw money at me and told me to be quiet. To never speak again about how he'd *lied* about me needing him. About him needing *me*. But I—I just couldn't get over what he had done. Abandon me once, shame on you. Abandon me twice, shame on me."

"But then you started working at Bellwether," Aiden said. "Didn't he know?"

Jenna nodded.

"Not at first. He isn't really hands-on—he leaves most of his work to his vice president. That useless, spineless man who would walk off a cliff if he asked. But eventually dear old Dad figured it out." She sighed. "I put on the performance of a lifetime, again, convincing him that I just so admired what he had done with the company and that, even though we didn't have a relationship, I would be happy enough working for him." She scoffed. "He ate that up."

Another breeze swept over them. Jenna closed her eyes to enjoy it.

When she opened them again, Aiden could see rage had surfaced.

"Then I realize he had been watching me. Keeping tabs so I wouldn't ruin his life. That's how it became so easy to bait him. The man would do anything to get more power, and I picked the perfect man for an affair, because he had that and money to spare. But." Her eyes narrowed at him. "But he was a fool to bring you in for help. You, a man who had a damn heart and wouldn't simply turn the other way. You took my chance to expose him. I wanted to make him sweat. I wanted to bleed him dry. I wanted to make him suffer, then watch him die, but, *no*, you had to bring other people in to try and do the right thing."

She took several steps forward. Aiden braced for a hit, but she stopped right in front of him. Her words were low and menacing.

"Leighton started digging until he needed Bryce's help. Then they dug so deep that they found me. And I couldn't let anyone find me. Not then, not now. Not ever."

Aiden knew then.

"You killed Bryce."

Jenna nodded.

"He wouldn't join my team, so I took him out of my game," she said. "Then I came for you next. But Leighton, bless his soul, really didn't like that."

Aiden went cold.

"What do you mean? Leighton isn't working with you?"

Jenna scoffed again.

"I sure thought I had persuaded him, but I guess he was still hung up on you." She put her hand on her hip and leaned back a little. Like she had decided relaxing was a normal thing at the moment. "Luckily, I already knew how to set him up to make everything that happened here, at the company and with you, look like an ex-lover's revenge."

That relaxation disappeared.

Then she looked annoyed.

"Even now while he's lying motionless in a hospital

bed, his hired hands are finishing his last task of killing your current boyfriend…all before coming for you." She sighed. "Ah, the story will be so big that no one will even think to look for the illegitimate child of Bellwether Tech."

Aiden's fear sent him straight to his own rage.

"You're wrong if you think someone won't put the truth together," he said. "Especially if you hurt Mack and his family. This town will look for you."

Jenna wagged her finger at him.

"That's what's so great about your failed office romance. Why look for me when they have Leighton?"

Aiden shook his head. This couldn't be happening.

"You can't do this," he tried instead.

But Jenna didn't seem at all put off.

Instead, she was back to her chipper smile.

Aiden didn't know what she had planned to say next because, a second later, all hell broke loose.

Chapter Twenty-One

No one had asked why Mack had become a bodyguard;
instead they had always asked what it was like. It was a
strange occupation for most to get their heads around, but
usually when they looked him up and down they thought it
made sense for him. He was a big, strong guy. Observant.
He had a thing about faces, too.

They also usually commented about him being a quiet
guy. Quiet people had patience, and patience was a virtue,
especially when it came to standing around usually waiting for nothing.

But Mack hadn't become a bodyguard because of his
skills or personality. No, Mack had become a bodyguard
because of Goldie.

It had been their father's birthday, and their mother had
come to town to celebrate with them. Their mom was a nice
woman, had been a kind mother, too, but after their dad had
died, something in her just broke. Finn had once admitted it
felt like they were always on thin ice around her, and then
one day they realized she had been the one standing on it,
not them. That ice had broken then and floated away with
her still on it. And, though they all cared about each other,
they hadn't gone after her, and she hadn't tried to come back.

Her leaving town was the reason Mack had come back to

town after college. The twins had just graduated from high school and had decided to make lives closer to home. Mack had wanted to show them that he was there, even though Willow Creek had been the last place he wanted to settle.

Goldie had known that. Finn had pretended he didn't.

Mack tried to be enthusiastic after returning, but he had become restless, aimless, too. The worst part: he hadn't realized it until one night a nineteen-year-old Goldie had come into his room with a folder in her hands.

"I want you to do a job for me," she had said. "Read through these and come out to the kitchen when you're done."

She had held it out to him with no more explanation then gone to wait. So, Mack had read through them. When he was done, he went to the kitchen.

"Are you serious about this?" he had asked, holding the folder up.

Goldie had nodded.

"If you're in, then I have some papers you need to sign." She had pointed to a stack of papers on the table, a ballpoint pen next to it. "Then we can talk details."

Mack had seen it then. Her seriousness. Her sincerity. Still, he didn't understand why her. Why him.

She had picked up on his one hesitation.

"I don't want a normal desk job, and you need to get out of this house," she had added.

It had been a simple answer, and that had been enough for Mack. He had signed the papers while Goldie explained what they meant at his side.

That was their first security contract, Mack as the bodyguard and Goldie as the boss.

Years later, their dynamic hadn't changed, and still no one had asked why he took on jobs to protect strangers.

It wasn't because he was big or strong. It wasn't because he was observant and had a thing with faces. He had done it because his sister had wanted him to leave his room.

It certainly hadn't been because he was patient.

Because, if there was one thing most people didn't know about his quiet, it was that it didn't suffer patience long.

That's why Mack didn't slow down for even an iota of time when he saw the man standing in front of the rooftop door.

Mack bulldozed up the last stairs and grabbed the man's wrist, pinned it back against his chest and slammed the man, his gun and Mack against the door with every bit of power he had.

Like Goldie's simple statement all those years ago, the simple move was more than enough.

The door exploded open, and the man yelled as he kept going backward. Mack still didn't let go. He didn't have to. He had already known the man was going to hit the ground hard. He also knew that he wouldn't be joining him.

Using his momentum and years of practice at keeping his balance in a fight, Mack used his hold on the man's arm to keep himself up while simultaneously driving the man down. Mack crouched as the man hit the graveled rooftop with a thud and crack. His eyes closed, and his body went slack. The hold he had on the gun loosened, and Mack took advantage.

He grabbed the gun and stood tall.

Mack didn't need to ask what the situation was. The second he saw Aiden standing opposite Jenna, he knew just by the man's stance who the villain was.

Mack lifted the gun and aimed it at the woman. He moved as he did so. She didn't seem to have a weapon, but when

Mack was close enough, he took Aiden's arm. He pulled him back and to his left. It put him out of the sight line of the door and put Mack between him and Jenna.

"I don't know what's going on, but I need you to stand real still," Mack ordered.

Jenna's eyes were wide, but she didn't seem afraid. She did, however, comply.

"Are you okay?" Mack didn't turn, but Aiden knew the question was for him.

"Yeah. I'm—I'm okay."

"Was there anyone else with you?"

"No. They brought me up here. With the gun you have."

Mack narrowed his eyes. Again, he didn't understand how Jenna factored into what was going on, but he sure as hell didn't care as long as he could keep Aiden safe.

"The two men who went to the basement. They're yours, too?"

Jenna wasn't smiling, but there was a twitch there. She had a gun on her, but she wasn't reacting the way she should.

"It's easier to get things done when you have helpers," she said. "All *three* of them."

It was subtle, but Mack caught it. An emphasis on the word *three*.

Her eyes flashed to the left.

That's when he knew he had made a mistake.

He had missed a guy.

Mack spun around and shot at the same time the fourth man sent off his own bullet. Both hits landed, but only one of them had someone they loved to protect. Aiden screamed out at him as Mack took his hit and walked forward for his second shot.

He had never been a fan of guns, but that didn't mean he hadn't been trained to use them.

Mack pulled the trigger with more accuracy than before.

He hoped Aiden wasn't looking, but he had to watch as the man fell in the doorway. He had to make sure he was down for the count.

"Mack!" Aiden was at his side but Mack wasn't going to let him stand in front again.

"Stay behind me," he ordered.

Aiden said something, but the sound was fading.

Mack managed to turn to Jenna.

"If you run, I'll shoot."

It was a bluff but, Mack would find out later, Jenna stayed stock-still regardless.

Which was good, because for the second time since meeting Aiden, Mack slipped into the darkness in his arms.

MACK WOKE UP on a Tuesday.

It was three in the morning and raining. Aiden was lying on the couch in his hospital room with a laptop on his stomach and the work he had tried to distract himself with untouched on the screen. At first he thought he was hearing things, but then Mack gave a little laugh.

Aiden nearly fell off the couch.

"Oh, God, you're awake." Aiden was a scrambling mess but managed to make it to Mack's bedside without destroying everything in the process.

Aiden didn't know what to do once he got there, so he did what felt right.

He put his hands on either side of Mack's face and then cried.

Mack watched for a few moments before his hand pressed over one of Aiden's. He patted it twice.

"I'm okay," he said, voice hoarse.

Aiden tried to get himself together while nodding.

"You are," he assured him. "You are."

Mack hadn't been, though. Not at all. He had been shot in the chest and had a total of three surgeries. His age, his good health and the other man's slightly bad aim had been the only reasons he had survived. The man who had shot him had not.

But Aiden wasn't going to tell him all that yet.

With great effort he slowed his crying and redirected his hold on to Mack's hand.

"Everyone else is okay, too," he said. "I'm supposed to get them the second you wake up."

Mack squeezed his hand.

"Stay here. For now."

Aiden didn't say no to that.

"Only if you promise to go back to sleep if you need to," he offered instead. "You're on some pretty good meds. The doctor said you might be sleepy for a while."

Mack nodded. The movement was sluggish. He was already fighting sleep again.

Aiden didn't stand in its way. He held Mack's hand until the man's eyes closed.

The worry in Aiden's chest finally lessened.

THE NEXT DAY Mack woke up again and, this time, managed to stay awake. Aiden had walked Mrs. Cole out to her car and missed his first moments, but he walked back in to find Ray talking his head off at the foot of his bed.

"Your sister is straight feral," he said. "I mean, I already knew she was, but the second Finn tore into the morgue and we realized we didn't have time to run, she made him get into one of the empty mortuary cabinets and *shut it*. Then, can you guess what that sister of yours did?"

Mack's bed had been situated so that he was sitting up. Aiden could easily see him smile.

"Jumped on the guys?"

Ray threw his arms up in total disbelief and awe.

"She jumped on the guys!" he exclaimed. "I mean, she was strategic about it, at least, and I was there to throw some equipment at them, but honestly, if I wasn't there, I think Goldie would have been fine."

Mack chuckled.

"Not many people know that for every self-defense and fighting class I took, Goldie went with me," he said. "If I remember correctly, we even tried to get you and mortuary cabinet Finn to come with us once. You two said you were busy."

Ray was just beside himself.

"Well, let me tell you what, I have reconsidered. Goldie has made me a believer. Go ahead and put me down as a yes to every single class in the future."

Mack was more than amused. Aiden could hear laughter in his one-word response.

"Deal."

Ray finally noticed Aiden had entered and waved him over to the spot where he had been sitting.

"I'll go get the wonder twins. You stay here and make sure this one doesn't get into any trouble."

Aiden agreed, and Ray was out of the room in a flash. When Aiden looked to Mack, the man was already staring.

"Did I dream it, or did you cry on me last night?" He was teasing. Aiden teased right back.

"Most people would pay good money to have someone as amazing as me crying over them, thank you very much."

"Is that so?"

Aiden crossed his arms over his chest and nodded deeply, once.

"That's very much so."

Mack held up one hand in defeat.

"Then you'll never hear me complain about Aiden Riggs crying over me again. Promise."

Aiden nodded.

"Good."

If it were up to him, Aiden would have continued joking around. It was already hard enough keeping himself from throwing his arms around Mack in relief. But Mack was a man who didn't like being in the dark. So, when he wanted to switch back to the serious, Aiden didn't fight it.

"Tell me what's happened since I've been out."

Aiden nodded again. He dropped his hands to his lap and began his recap. He started with what Jenna had told him on the rooftop and then what happened right after Mack had been shot.

"Detective Winters was the one who showed up before anyone could get a call out of the hospital for deputies. He wasn't too far behind you, actually. He cuffed Jenna and helped me carry you off the rooftop. It wasn't until you were already being taken to surgery that the rest of the department showed." Mack was obviously surprised at that. Aiden had been, too, until the detective had explained once everything had calmed down.

"Winters said that he knew he was missing a lot of information, but the thing that bothered him the most was Jonathan Smith," Aiden said. "The more he thought about it, he believed that Jonathan had been told to go after me by someone else. So, he went to visit him as soon as the county jail opened and confronted him. Apparently, Jonathan caved. He had been paid by a man to grab and take me to a rental home in Willow Creek where I could lie low for a few days until some kind of mess was sorted out."

"You mean—"

"He was supposed to take me to Bluebird Breeze. But, instead, he had been so nervous about it all that he had gone a little overboard. He was trying to make me pass out so I wouldn't fight him. Unlucky for him, a certain bodyguard just happened to be obsessed with me."

Aiden grinned.

Mack rolled his eyes.

"On with the story there, Mr. Riggs."

Aiden laughed but then became serious again. He didn't know how to feel about the next part. He wouldn't for a long while.

"Leighton was the one who paid him. That's why Winters rushed here, especially when he realized that I was here, too. You apparently made such a fuss going up to the roof that he knew to hightail it there, too."

"Leighton wanted you to go to Bluebird Breeze," Mack underlined.

Aiden nodded. He recounted the story that Leighton himself had told Aiden two days ago while Mack had still been sleeping.

"After you left the company, I was promoted," he had told Aiden. *"I'd been working hard for years to get there, so when the CEO told me that he had learned from his mistakes, I took his word. But then it happened again a few months later. Bryce was called in to loop a video, erase some other footage and keep quiet about it. Bryce didn't like that, and instead of coming to me to talk it out, he as-*

*sumed I was part of it. It wasn't until two weeks ago that
I realized he was going to go public with the information.
And, not only that, he was going to Willow Creek to find
you to help him do it. Bryce was a smart guy, but you're
the one with the better skills."*

Aiden had told him that Bryce had never gotten in touch
with him.

At this Leighton had frowned so completely Aiden was
almost moved to sympathy.

*"I didn't want you to be involved. Even though you
hacked into different databases in the name of good, what
you did wasn't exactly legal. So when I realized Bryce was
in town, I asked to meet him so we could talk about a way
to leave you out of everything. But, when I went there, I
found Jenna instead."*

Jenna had made herself known as the CEO's daughter
then and given Leighton the same rundown she had given
Aiden on the roof, as far as Aiden could tell. Then she had
given Leighton the same choice she had Bryce.

*"She wanted me to help dismantle Bellwether Tech
but do it her way. She had the money, she had the power,
she just didn't have the technical know-how. Plus, Holloway had always been suspicious of her. She also wanted
you."* Leighton had shaken his head at that. *"I told her you
weren't needed, but she already knew that you had been the
one to find out about the blackmail. She said if we couldn't
use you, she would kill you. I knew she was serious, so I
acted fast. And clumsily."*

Leighton had sent Jonathan to try and take Aiden out
of the equation. But then Mack had shown up. After that,
Jenna had made her move with the four hired helpers she
had been using for years for her own nefarious deeds.

*"After Mack helped you out of that again, I had to figure
out a way to separate you two. I didn't realize that Jenna
had already decided to make me the fall guy."*

"The laptop at Bluebird Breeze," Aiden had guessed.
"She set that up."

Leighton had nodded.

*"Then I started to build a case against her until I heard
she had gone to Willow Creek. I knew she was going to tie
up our loose end—you—and, since I wasn't sure where
her guys were, I panicked and tried to take away the reason why I couldn't hide you until I could figure out a plan
that worked."*

*"You were trying to shoot Mack when you came to my
house. Not me."*

*"I didn't want to kill him, just make him stop getting in
the way so I could save you."*

Aiden had become angry then. Angrier than he ever had
been.

Leighton didn't try to apologize.

"For what it's worth, I'm glad he's okay," was all he
had said instead.

After that, Aiden had given him only one last courtesy
before leaving for good.

"For what it's worth, I'm glad you're okay, too."

That was the last time he saw Leighton and, even though
it hurt, Aiden felt better having gotten his side of the story.

Mack had, too.

"I guess I can't get too mad at him," he said now. "He
might not have gone about it the right way, but he was just
trying to protect someone he cared about. I get that."

Aiden's cheeks had burned a little at that.

Then he sighed.

"All this trouble went nowhere." Aiden took Mack's hand in his. "Caleb Holloway passed away three days ago due to his injuries from the accident. His funeral was yesterday."

Aiden hadn't known how to feel about that piece of news, either. Mack, in the moment, took it okay.

"I would have liked to talk to him," he admitted.

In the weeks to come, Mack and his siblings would talk to Jenna while she awaited trial. There the Atwoods would get confirmation that Caleb had told his daughter he had started the fire to ruin their father. When he had realized it had instead trapped him inside, he hadn't tried to help him escape. Caleb Holloway hadn't purposely killed their father, but he had purposely not saved him. In that way, the four of them had shared a moment of true disgust for a man who had been known to the public as a promoter of safety and security and compassion. After that, none of them saw Jenna again.

But in the hospital room, once Mack had been caught up as much as Aiden could help with, the two of them had simply sighed.

"I think it would be really nice if we could not visit the hospital for a while," Aiden said. "I heard one of the doctors joke that we're starting to be frequent fliers."

Mack laughed.

He was still holding Aiden's hand.

"It would be nice to go out and see other places together, too. Maybe do something with a slower pace. I know this might be old-fashioned, but dinner and a movie might be fun."

Aiden thought he was going along with the bit, but Mack squeezed his hand. His expression softened.

"What do you say, Mr. Potted Plant?"

Heat rose up into Aiden's face, but he smiled.

"Are you asking me out on date from your hospital bed?"

Mack nodded.

"I've been told I might not be romantic, but I'll let you know, I'm impatient. I need an answer now. Please and thank you."

Aiden couldn't help but laugh.

"Call me a potted plant again and we'll see if I go anywhere with you."

Mack didn't argue, and two weeks later they were sitting front and center at the movie theater. Mack had the popcorn in one hand, and Aiden's hand in the other. Before the movie started, Mack leaned over and whispered.

"Be thankful this isn't an art exhibit."

Aiden turned his head, confused.

But Mack wasn't in the mood to explain. As soon as Aiden's lips were there, Mack's were right there, too.

The kiss was long and deep.

Aiden knew the movie must have started but, for the life of him, he didn't seem to care.

* * * * *